Family Is Everything

Dollie James Jamerson

JamerSun Publishing, LLC

JamerSun Publishing, LLC
Canton, Michigan

ISBN-13: 978-1-7370816-7-8

Library of Congress Control Number: 2025917066

Edited by Angela R. Edwards
www.pearlygatespublishing.com

Printed in the United States of America

Family Is Everything

Early one morning, around 4:30, I was awakened by my neighbor's dog barking. I lay in bed thinking, "Oh, my God! What is he barking at?" Suddenly, the patio's motion-sensor light flicked on, shining brightly through the bedroom window. I slowly eased out of bed, looking for the source of the sudden disturbance, only to find a deer standing by the big tree in my yard. *"Oh! That's why the dog is barking,"* I thought. I stayed in place, silently watching the deer until it finally moved out of view of the light, happy when the dog ceased its incessant barking and the light went off.

As I stood there, gazing into the darkness, I remembered a conversation with Mrs. Diaz where she mentioned a deer had fallen into her pool, and they had a hard time getting it out. Three weeks later, when I came home from work, I noticed they had installed a privacy fence around their backyard. After our recent deer visit, I thought we needed fencing as well. I didn't want a deer to fall into our pool or accidentally run through the patio window. Just the thought of the latter made me shiver.

Eventually, I climbed back into bed and looked over at my husband, who was sound asleep. I couldn't believe he slept through the dog barking! Unfortunately for me, my mind was all over the place, rendering me unable to fall back asleep. I rested my head against the headboard, closed my eyes, prayed, and then reminisced about the past. The orange and yellow morning skies beyond the window provided me with a sweet moment of relief.

****

Let me introduce myself. I am Amber Rose Crayton-Hollinger, a minister of God's Word, Family and Public Offender

Lawyer, and mother of two. I am happily married to Bryce Hollinger, a God-fearing man and Navy recruiting officer who has served for 12 years. Our daughter's name is Kyra, and our son is Bryce Jr., but we call him BJ.

Kyra's father is Carl Benson. He and I were seniors in high school who shared a few classes. I didn't know him very well at first; he was just a boy in my class. Carl was also the captain of the football team, handsome, and very popular with the girls. As prom approached, he asked me to be his date. I was thrilled and quickly accepted. On the night of the prom, I had a great time dancing and enjoying myself with my friends. Later, as he drove me home, he said he wanted to show me a place where he often went to look out over the city. As we sat there, looking at the lights and talking, he suddenly overpowered me and forced himself on me. I was horrified and wished that night could just disappear from my memory.

Sadly, my wish didn't come true. Two months later, I discovered I was pregnant. When I told Carl, it didn't faze him at all. In fact, his response was, "None of the other girls I went out with ever told me anything like that." It was evident that he didn't care, and I chose to remain silent about the whole ordeal.

On our graduation day, another tragic incident happened. I was in a bathroom stall when three or four cheerleaders entered. I heard them talking about a bet some of the football players made on how many girls they could sleep with before graduation. My name and Monica Green's name were mentioned among a few others. I stayed in the stall, listening to more of their conversation. They discussed the colleges they would attend and engaged in some casual chitchat. One of them said, "Ky Green, Carl Benson, and Corey Jones got a full-ride scholarship to Michigan State. They'll be leaving in July. I've been accepted there, too. I plan on staying with my mom's sister." As they kept talking, I thought back to their earlier conversation. Did I hear right when they said Monica's name? How was I going to tell my Mama that I was pregnant by a boy who was going off to college and hadn't even believed me when I told him?

After graduation, I enrolled in the university, taking 12 hours of pre-classes. I also worked at the salon with my mother in the afternoons and on weekends. One day, while shopping at Walmart, I ran into Monica Green. She was there to get some supplies for college. We talked for a while, and that's when I learned she'd start classes at Mississippi State in late August. Neither of us mentioned what happened during prom night, although it stayed at the forefront of my mind, mainly because I was pregnant with Carl's baby. When the fall semester started, I took a full course load of 21 credit hours.

For the first six months of my pregnancy, my Mama didn't notice my growing belly. When she finally discovered my "situation," she was disappointed but supportive... up to a certain point. Kyra was born on a Wednesday night in October. She was a beautiful baby with a full head of hair and was my pride and joy. Everybody said she looked just like me. The following Wednesday, I was back in school, determined to earn my degree and provide a wonderful life for my daughter and myself. I hadn't heard from or seen Carl until Kyra was four months old. At that time, he was home from college. He stopped by and said that one of his friends told him I had a baby and was going around telling everyone he was the father. After that brief visit and continued denial, I never heard from him again.

Mama loved Kyra, but she didn't go back on her word. She said she would watch the baby for me when I went to class—nothing more. I remember when my friend and I wanted to see the movie *Black Panther*. The night we decided to go, Mama said she wouldn't keep the baby, so I took her with us. As soon as the lights went down in the theater, Kyra started crying and making so much noise that I was asked to leave. That same night, Mama came into my room, stood over my bed, and prayed for me. Then, she walked over to Kyra's crib, placed her hand on Kyra's head, and prayed for her, asking God to protect her and to save me.

One day, while I was washing dishes in the kitchen, Mama came in and asked, "Amber, if the Lord came back today, would you be ready to go back with Him?"

I stood there, trying to find an answer in my mind, but couldn't think of one. "I don't know" was my reply.

"You need to know," Mama said. 'If you confess with your mouth and believe in your heart that God has raised Jesus from the dead, you can be saved." That night, I committed my life to the Lord. Mama gave me a Bible with my name on it and encouraged me to read it every day and pray. As I continued to read my Bible and pray, God's Word became alive in my life. That's when things started to change for the better. While still attending school, I got a job working at a law firm. After I graduated three years later, I took and passed the bar exam. The Lord blessed me with a full-time job there.

When Kyra was two and a half years old, we moved to the Astro subdivision at 2206 Red Bird Circle Drive. There were 11 houses around the circle, with ours positioned in the center. Our home featured five bedrooms, four bathrooms, and a two-car garage, along with a swimming pool and patio in the backyard. One day, the subdivision held a block club meeting, where I met my neighbors. Everyone attended except for one lady with two small children who were out of town. Kyra and I were warmly welcomed to the neighborhood, and it was mentioned that all the neighbors looked out for each other. The residents on our circle were an eclectic mix of professionals: two schoolteachers, an electrician, two stay-at-home mothers, two older women, a police officer who hosted the meeting, and a woman who ran a daycare.

When Kyra turned three, I hosted a birthday party for her and invited all the children in the neighborhood. I rented a bounce house and a water slide for the celebration. One of the lawyers I work with had a farm and brought her two children and two horses with her.

That's when I finally met the woman who was out of town during the block meeting. She lived in the first house in the circle. Her name was Olivia Williams. She was a high school counselor who moved from Bay City, Michigan, a year before I moved into my house. She actually had three children, but the oldest boy, Marcus, lived in Bay City with her mother, while the other two lived with her. Zoe was a little younger than Kyra, and Carlos was a one-year-old.

As time went on, Olivia and I became best friends. She would babysit Kyra for me from time to time, and I would watch her children when needed. She didn't say much about her children's father, but when she did, she called him 'Morgan,' said he lived out of state, and that he wanted to move back to Dallas with her, despite having a good job as an electrician. For visitations, they met halfway twice a month, and on holidays, she and her two children would fly to see Morgan.

****

As I looked over at my sleeping husband, I couldn't help but smile when I remembered the day this handsome, God-fearing, romantic man entered my life. I recall sitting in the middle pew at church, looking back, when a tall, handsome man in a Navy uniform walked in. An older lady accompanied him. He sat on the other side of the church, also in the middle pew, across from me. The lady continued walking to the front and sat beside the pastor's wife. When I shyly looked in the man's direction, I saw him looking back at me, smiling, and then subtly waving hello. I smiled and waved back.

I returned my focus to the front of the church, thinking about how, just a few months earlier, I had consecrated myself and fasted three days a week during September, drinking only water. During that time, I prayed and asked God to send me a man who loved Him and would love my daughter and me. I also prayed that He would bless me with more work and money to help pay my bills. I sat there pondering, "Why is this man looking at me? Is he one of my prayers being answered?"

After church, the mystery man approached me. My heart was racing! The first thing he asked after introducing himself as Bryce Hollinger was, "Are you married?"

"No, I'm not," I answered quickly.

"Are you in a relationship?"

Another quick answer: "No. Why all the questions?"

He smiled and replied, "The Lord told me to come to church today and that you would be waiting for me."

"He did?" I asked, completely blown away by the transparency of his response in relation to my prayers.

"Yes, He did."

I stood there, looking at him, captivated by his brownish-grey eyes and smooth medium-brown complexion. "Oh, my God! He's so handsome! You sent him here for me, God?" were my thoughts.

We talked for a while as if we had known each other for years. He introduced me to his mother, who was my pastor's wife's aunt. When Kyra walked over, I introduced her to them. Before parting ways, Bryce asked me to put my number in his phone. After doing so, he then said, "You will be hearing from me," as he flashed his gorgeous smile.

As Kyra and I drove home, she asked, "Mama, that man and lady were nice, weren't they?"

"Yes, they were," I assured her.

Bryce called later that night and every day until it was time for him to return to duty. That Saturday, on his way to the airport for his flight to Connecticut, he stopped by our house to say goodbye. It was a bittersweet moment, but I understood that he was active-duty military and couldn't stay any longer.

Then, on the Wednesday of the following week, I checked my bank account before paying Kyra's daycare bill. To my surprise, the IRS had deposited my tax refund, totaling $7,725.25. I sat in my living room and cried, thanking God for the money to cover my bills. I knew without a doubt that my prayers were being answered.

When Bryce returned to base, he called me and said, "You're going to be my wife. I already spoke with my mom and told her I'm going to marry you." In response, his mother said, "She's a beautiful young lady. I would love to have her as my daughter and that little girl as my granddaughter." He laughed when he told me his Mama was ready to bake our wedding cake!

It became routine for Bryce to call twice a week to talk to Kyra and me, but that was until two weeks had passed without a word from him. I missed talking to him and wondered if he was alright. Four weeks later, he called and said he was out at sea and couldn't call. That was also the first time he told me he loved me. "Amber, how do you feel about me?" he asked.

"You are my knight in shining armor. The only difference is that you entered the church wearing a Navy uniform instead of riding a white horse across the great Mississippi River," I replied.

He chuckled at my comparison and asked, "Where in the world did you get that from?"

"The movie *Queens*," I said matter-of-factly.

Bryce kept laughing and then said, "I gotta go now. I love you."

Three months before his discharge from the Navy, a special delivery box arrived at my house. It was a medium-sized box, and inside, there was a smaller box with an engagement ring and a simple note that read, "Will you marry me?" I thought that was so romantic. The ring was beautiful, with a large diamond and smaller diamonds all around the band.

As if he somehow knew the exact moment, I opened the box, Bryce called and asked, "Did you receive a box?"

"Yes. I just opened it."

"Well, what is your answer?" he persisted.

"Yes, Bryce! Yes, I will marry you!"

I could hear the joy in his voice when he said, "I need to call Mama and let her know we're getting married when I get home!"

Two months after Bryce returned, we got married in the same church where we first met. It was a beautiful wedding. My Mama and Aunt Edna flew in from Virginia, and Bryce's brother and sister drove in from Alabama. I invited all my neighbors. Olivia was my maid of honor, and Kyra was my flower girl. After the wedding, Bryce and I flew to Las Vegas for our honeymoon. Mama and Aunt Edna watched Kyra for me. Ten months later, BJ was born, and Bryce adopted Kyra.

After I got married and BJ was born, Olivia and I didn't see each other as often as we used to, but we talked on the phone almost every day. Plus, either her children were at my house or Kyra was at hers. One early Friday morning, Olivia called me to ask for prayer. During that call, she also asked if I could watch her children for a few days because she had to go out of town, but she would explain everything when she got back. I agreed, thinking she was going to meet up with her children's father.

Four days passed, and Olivia's children were still at my house without any word from her. That Friday afternoon, while hosting her son Carlos's sixth birthday party, my cellphone rang. On the other end was a woman crying hysterically, saying, "This is Olivia's mother, Carina. Olivia died a few minutes ago! My baby is dead!" Needless to say, I was in shock. Ms. Carina went on to explain, "I met her at the cancer treatment center in Cleveland, Ohio. Her body was too weak for the extensive treatment." My tears joined with hers. "I must fly her body back there to make the final arrangements. Will you keep the children until I arrive? I have already called Olivia's son, Marcus, and the children's father. They will meet me at her house." I told her I would keep the children for her and not to worry about them. I heard her heartbreaking wails as she hung up the phone. I called Bryce inside and explained what happened. "How am I going to tell the children that their mom's dead?"

"You don't tell them anything. They must hear it from their grandmother," he replied.

When I shared the news with our neighbors, they were all shocked to hear about Olivia's sudden passing. On Saturday, around 6:00 p.m., I received a call from Ms. Carina, who told me I could send the children home and explained that Marcus and the children's father would arrive Sunday night. After church on Sunday, I stopped by with dinner for them and told Ms. Carina to call me if she needed anything.

On the day of Olivia's memorial service, all our neighbors came to show their support. As the family entered to view her body, I saw Carl Benson, Kyra's biological father. I couldn't believe my eyes! I wondered whether he knew the family well or if he had moved back to Dallas. After the service, members of the church prepared food for the repast for the family at the community center next to the church.

Kyra and I sat at a table with Carlos, Zoe, and Ms. Carina. At one point, Carl came over and sat next to Carlos on the other side of the table, facing us. When he looked across the table, he was surprised to see me. "Amber Crayton? Is that you?"

"Yes, it is."

"Then that must be Kyra. She's beautiful, looking just like you."

"When did you get back into town, Carl? I haven't seen or heard from you in over eight years," I said sharply.

"I made it in four days ago with Marcus and a couple of Olivia's family members," he replied hesitantly.

"Oh! So, you know the family?" I asked curiously.

He looked at Carlos and Zoe before saying, "These are my children, Amber."

"They're your children?" I asked, totally surprised.

"Yes. Olivia and I weren't married, but these are our children. We met in college. When we graduated, I moved to Bay City with her. After being together for a year, she received a call about a job here in Dallas. We were planning to get married next

June, but then this happened." As he spoke, tears ran down his cheeks. I told him I'd known Olivia for over five years and that when she talked about her children's father, she called him Morgan. "That's my middle name," he replied.

I sat there thinking, *"I knew Olivia all these years and never knew her children were my daughter's brother and sister. Their last name is Williams, not Benson. There was no way I would've made the connection without someone telling me."*

His eyes were fixated on Kyra when he asked me, "So, what are you doing these days?"

"I'm a Family and Public Offender Lawyer."

"A lawyer? Wow!"

While I was talking with Ms. Carina, I noticed Carl whispering across the table to Kyra. I heard her say, "My daddy is at home."

"No, he's not. I'm your real daddy. Ask your Mama," he said, turning his attention to me.

"Why did you tell her that?" I whispered to him through clenched teeth. We stared each other down, with me shaking my head, hoping he would shut his mouth and stop talking to Kyra altogether.

Just then, a woman approached, whom Ms. Carina introduced as Olivia's Aunt Ruth. She explained that I was the neighbor who looked after Olivia's children for her. I politely shook her hand and said she could have my seat, as my daughter and I were getting ready to leave. I was so disgusted with Carl for taking it upon himself to share something that was not his place to share with Kyra. I embraced Ms. Carina and told her I would be praying for her. I also extended the offer for her to feel free to call me at any time. I also hugged Carlos and Zoe before grabbing Kyra's hand and leaving.

During our ride home, Kyra asked the question I feared. "Mama, is that man really my daddy?" I couldn't lie to her, so I told her about him while leaving out what he did to me. The confusion was evident on her face when she asked, "Then, who is daddy at home?" I then explained Bryce's role in her life, which led to yet another question. "Mama, did you love that man?"

"No, baby. I knew nothing about love back then. Things just happened, and I got pregnant with you. Then, he went away to Michigan to play football. It's been years since I last heard from him." Kyra listened quietly without saying another word for the rest of the trip home.

As soon as we entered the house, she went straight to the family room to tell Bryce that she had met a man that day who claimed to be her father. Bryce was genuinely surprised but hugged her and asked, "Oh, you did? What did you think about that?"

"Nothing, because you are my daddy," she said, hugging him tightly before heading to her room.

"So, Kyra's birth father was at the memorial service?" Bryce asked.

"Yes, he was there. All these years later, I thought I would never see that man again, but there he was!" I continued to share everything Carl had told me, along with the details Olivia had shared about "her children's father," never once revealing that his real name was Carl Benson.

Bryce looked at me with genuine concern and asked, "How did you feel when you saw him?"

"I don't know… Shocked. Surprised. I could have punched him dead in the face for telling Kyra about him being her father. He told her other things, like he's been in her life all the time. What he should have told her was how he abandoned her before she was born." I stopped talking and looked at Bryce contemplatively. "Why did you ask me that?"

"I just asked," he answered plainly.

I desperately needed to change the subject. "I know one thing: we need to pray for those children. They found it very hard to see their mother lying in that casket. Did you and BJ eat anything yet?"

"Yes, we went to Golden Corral," he said, rising from his seat. "Let me go peek in at my daughter, then I'm going to bed." He turned and asked, "Are you coming?"

"No. Not yet. I'll be up in a little while."

Bryce must have heard the distress in my voice because he came over, pulled me up from my seat, embraced me warmly, and said, "Kyra is my daughter. I don't care what that man says, and I don't want to hear anything else about it." He then kissed my forehead and went into Kyra's room.

A week later, a moving truck pulled up to Olivia's house. That afternoon, Zoe and Carlos came over to tell us they were moving to Bay City to live with their father and grandmother. Zoe asked if Kyra could come to their house while they packed. Bryce said it was okay, as long as BJ went with her. When they returned home, Kyra said, "Zoe's daddy said he wants me to come to Bay City and visit them sometimes because they are my family, too. He gave me his phone number and this picture of him," handing the small photo to Bryce.

★★★★★★★★★★★★★★★★★★★★

That reminiscent moment was interrupted when I heard Bryce saying, "Amber! Amber! Why are you sitting up sleeping?" as he rubbed my thigh.

"I'm not asleep," I replied. I then told him about the deer and suggested that we put a fence in the backyard. "I thought you were asleep, Bryce."

"No, I wasn't. I'm just lying here, looking at my beautiful wife, thinking of how you make me feel," he said, laughing as he pulled me down to lie next to him. "You know, tomorrow, the children will be leaving for the youth retreat. Honestly, I'm not ready for that separation."

"Kyra is ten, and BJ is six. They will be okay," I said confidently. "Plus, your Mom is going. She and a few other mothers prepared the food for them."

He started to laugh and said, "Now, I'm feeling better by letting them go with Mama there."

That Friday at noon, the children left for the weekend retreat. Friday night, Bryce and I watched a movie on TV, snacked on popcorn, played hide-and-seek in the house, and enjoyed being childless for the weekend. Saturday morning, we went out for breakfast and then headed to the mall to buy summer clothes for BJ.

"Kyra is too picky for me to choose her clothes," Bryce admitted. "You will have to bring her shopping when she gets back home. Do you remember when you had that trial in Lancaster, and every store we went into, she didn't see anything she liked? When I told her I was ready to go empty-handed, that's when she said, 'Dad, let's go back to Justice. I think I saw something in there I liked.' Did you know she went back and picked up the first outfit I told her would look nice on her?" He was laughing so hard. "Even BJ is tired of her! So, you can shop for her, and I'll shop for BJ. How about that?"

At that moment, we were both laughing uncontrollably. Bryce decided to shop for BJ and himself, while I chose outfits for Kyra. As we kept walking through the mall, we looked for a jewelry store because we wanted to buy something for our seventh wedding anniversary on Sunday. Suddenly, someone came up from behind and snatched Bryce's cap off his head. We turned around to see a lady standing there, holding his cap and laughing. He looked surprised when he realized who it was.

"Bryce! I thought that was you," the woman said as Bryce reached for his cap.

"Sarah, why did you do that?" he asked irritably.

She walked toward him with her arms open for a hug, but Bryce stepped back. "Nice to see you, too," she said sarcastically while laughing. "Oh. This must be the wifey."

"Yes, she is. Amber, this is Sarah."

I spoke to her, but she just looked me up and down.

Instead of recognizing my kindness, she bitterly said, "I dated Bryce. Did he tell you that? He left me, went into the Navy, and never bothered to call or write." As Bryce and I stood there dumbfounded, she started yelling. "I lost my baby and fell into depression, Bryce! I watched you buying boys' clothes today, and my baby is dead!"

A woman was standing beside her, gently trying to coax her away. "Sarah, let's go."

"You were wrong for leaving me, Bryce. I didn't even know where you were!" Sarah cried as the woman pulled her away to sit on a nearby bench.

Throughout the entire ordeal, I stood beside my husband, rubbing his back. Not once did he respond to Sarah's accusations. Finally, we turned and walked away. We entered Zale's jewelry store, where Bryce bought a necklace with a cross for himself and a set for me, but mine was smaller with a diamond in the center. As we left the mall, both of us remained silent. I know he was thinking about what Sarah said. I definitely was.

When we got home, Bryce kissed me and said, "I love you, Amber. I have enjoyed being married to you these past seven years. The Lord made you just for me." Then he went into his office to pray and read his Bible. I prayed, took a shower, and climbed into bed. Around 9:30, he showered and got into bed, pulling me close. He whispered in my ear, "Did you say your prayers?"

"Yes, I said my prayers and prayed for you, too."

"All that Sarah said today was news to me. I feel sorry for her. Before I left for the Navy, I hadn't seen her in over a year. If she were pregnant, there was no way that child was mine. How are you feeling about what you heard today?"

"I think something is wrong with her mind. Losing her child must have been hard on her, and seeing you buy clothes for another child probably reminded her of the baby she lost. She's angry and confused. I truly feel sorry for her," I replied.

"Amber, you are the best wife. I knew when I married you that I'd obtain favor from the Lord. Do you really love me?"

"Yes, Bryce. I really love you."

"Happy seventh anniversary eve," he said, planting a sweet kiss on my lips.

After church on Sunday, when the children returned from the retreat, they were excited as they told us about the event. Kyra told us that grandmom kept BJ with her because he wouldn't follow directions. That was hilarious to Bryce, who replied, "I knew Mama wasn't going to let him get away with anything!" Later that evening, we all went out for our anniversary dinner.

The first three weeks after the retreat, the children stayed with Bryce's mother. After a while, they started complaining, saying there was nothing to do there. Bryce began taking BJ to work with him, and Kyra came to work with me on the days she wasn't volunteering at the daycare center down the street from our house.

One Wednesday morning, while I was at work reviewing a case for that afternoon, my secretary called and said there was someone here to see me. "I don't have anyone scheduled to see me today," I replied.

"She says her name is Ms. Manatee," came the reply.

I chuckled and said, "I have never had an appointment with anyone by that name. Did she say what it's about?"

"No. She just asked to speak to you."

Over the intercom, I heard the visitor say, "Tell her it's important."

I recognized the voice immediately as Sarah's. *"Oh, my God. Why is she here to see me?"* I thought. I told my secretary to give me 15 minutes and then bring her back. After ending the call, I prayed, "Lord, give me the right words to say to this lady. I thank You that Kyra didn't come to work with me today. Amen." I then called Bryce and told him Sarah was at my office.

"She's in your office with you right now?" he asked, concerned.

"No. I told my secretary to wait 15 minutes and then bring her back."

"Is Kyra with you?"

"No, she's at the daycare today."

"Okay. I'll leave BJ here at the job. I'm on my way."

Fifteen minutes later, my secretary knocked on the door and entered with Sarah. As my secretary walked out, I asked her to leave the door open and asked Ms. Manatee to have a seat. She sat and looked around my office with a curious eye. "Ms. Manatee, why are you here to see me?" I asked.

"Call me Sarah."

"Okay. Sarah, why are you here to see me?"

She didn't respond. Instead, she just kept looking around the room, eventually asking for a bottle of water. I walked to my small refrigerator to retrieve the water. Before I could turn and hand it to her, she said, "I changed my mind. I don't want anything to drink."

"Sarah, I must ask again: Why are you here?"

She stood, looked at the family photo on my desk, then directly at me, and said, "You need to let him go. Bryce is my man. You're a pretty lady. You can find someone else."

I looked up and saw Bryce standing in the doorway behind her. Sarah noticed I was looking past her, so she turned around and saw Bryce staring at her angrily. "Why are you here, Sarah?"

Sarah flashed a big smile as she walked toward him. "I knew you would come to get me." She had her arms open to give him a hug. "I came here to tell your wife to leave you alone. She's a lovely lady, but she needs to find someone else. Then, we can be together."

Bryce had a frown on his face when he said, "Sarah, I am not leaving my wife for you."

"My baby died!" she yelled through a flood of tears. "Died, Bryce!"

"Sarah, I'm sorry for the loss of your baby, but you need to leave," he replied sternly.

She focused on a spot on the carpet in front of her. "Rob told me he loved me, and he's gone, too." She then started to cry loudly. I could tell she had mental health issues by her behavior.

Bryce asked a question both of us needed an answer to: "Sarah, how did you know where my wife worked?"

Through her tears, she said, "When I saw you at the mall, I followed you home."

"What? You followed us home?" he shouted.

"Yes, I did. And two weeks ago, I sat on the corner in my car near your street and watched her leave," she continued, pointing at me. "She dropped off those two children," she said, pointing at the family photo.

I thought, *"Oh, my God! She knows where we and Bryce's mother live!"*

Sarah continued. "Monday, I followed her, and she came here. I decided to come in today to tell her to leave you alone."

I could tell Bryce was upset when she said she followed me to my workplace. He looked at me and said, "Babe, call security to have this lady escorted out of here." Then he turned to Sarah and said, "You need help. Leave my family and me alone."

Suddenly, Sarah's tears stopped, and she burst out laughing as she walked out and slammed the door behind her.

Bryce sat in the nearest chair, put his head in his hands, and whispered, "Lord, I don't believe this." He stayed with me for a while, giving Sarah time to leave the property. After some time, he stood and said, "I'm going back to work to pick up BJ, then I'm going home." He came over to me, hugged me, and kissed me on my forehead. As he was leaving, he called back over his shoulder, "I hope that lady's gone."

Thankfully, weeks passed without Sarah's appearance or contact.

****

The second week of August, Bryce and I took the children to Disney World. One of the lawyers who works in the building with me met us there with her family. Both of our families had a great time during the trip.

When we got back home, I took Bryce to pick up his car from the recruiting office. To our dismay, someone had spray-painted his silver Charger with blue paint. "Oh, my God! Who would do something like that?" I asked, already suspecting who it might be.

Bryce sat there, looking at the damage to his car. I knew he was upset. "Babe, I should have listened to you and driven my car home to park it in the garage, but I thought it would be safe here."

"Things like this happen," I replied, not hiding the anger in my own voice.

"Who wants to ride home with me and my newly decorated car?" he asked the children while laughing.

"I will ride with you, daddy. We can stop by Burger King and get me a burger. I'm hungry!" Kyra volunteered.

"I'm coming, too!" BJ said as he climbed out of the SUV.

"Oh, great. So, everybody is deserting me?" I joked.

"BJ, ride with Mama. We'll all stop at Burger King," Bryce said with a smile.

We got our food, drove home, and when we finished eating, Bryce told the children to take their showers and then come back down so we could pray and thank God for a safe trip home. He then called his mom to let her know we were back. After our prayer, I took a shower and climbed into bed while Bryce stayed up talking with the children.

As Bryce got into bed, he said, "I wonder if it was Sarah who spray-painted my car."

"We were gone for over a week. Anybody could have done that. It was probably some kids," I replied, trying not to voice my suspicions about Sarah.

"I'll look at the surveillance camera on Monday when I get to work."

Monday afternoon, when he got home from work, he told me that the surveillance camera showed some boys bouncing a ball around his car one day, and then the next day, he saw someone near his vehicle but couldn't tell who it was. "Now, I have to repaint my whole car," he said with a sad face. I had to laugh at his silly gesture. He threw me on the bed, kissed me, and said, "Stop laughing at me! It's not funny!" That made me laugh even harder. He's so hilarious!

When the children's school year started, my workload increased, and Bryce was out of town at the recruiting office in Tyler, Texas, for three weeks. While he was away, he called and FaceTimed us every afternoon. Before hanging up, we would pray, and he would tell us he loved and missed us.

One day, while commuting to work, I found myself counting down the days until Bryce's return home—only four more days. During that period, I was assigned to handle a custody hearing involving three children. The trial was set to begin at 3:30 that afternoon, so I texted Kyra and told her to get off the bus at Grandmom's house. I left the courthouse around 5:00 p.m. and went straight to Bryce's mother's house to pick up the children.

When they got in the car, Kyra asked, "Mama, why did you tell us to go to Grandmom's house and then send a lady to the school to pick us up?"

"What? I didn't send anyone to pick you guys up!"

"Well, this lady said that you wanted her to pick us up and take us to McDonald's to get something to eat, and that she would keep us until you got home."

I couldn't believe what I was hearing. "Kyra, what did the lady look like?" She described the woman to me, adding that she wore a brown coat with a fur collar. "A fur collar?" I asked.

"Yes," Kyra replied.

"Mama, she had on shower shoes and dark glasses, too," BJ added.

While they talked, I pulled into the garage, and the children went into the house. I stayed in my car, thinking about what the children said. My mind immediately went to the lady I saw in court earlier that day. When I finally went inside, I asked the children, "Why didn't you go with that lady?"

"Because you told us to go to Grandmom's house," Kyra replied. "But BJ wanted to go with her. I had to keep pulling him back. Then the bus came."

While she was speaking, I thought about Friday, when I was making my closing arguments in court, and I noticed a woman sitting in the courtroom wearing dark glasses and a brown coat with a fur collar. I saw the same woman today. Could she be Sarah stalking me and trying to kidnap my children? "I'm so happy you guys didn't go with that lady," I said, giving them a hug. I then settled in the living room, waiting for Bryce to call me, but he was taking too long, so I called him.

He answered the phone immediately, saying, "Babe, I know I'm running late calling you. My recruit just left. I was just about to call. How is everybody?"

"Sarah went to our children's school and tried to get them to leave with her."

"She did what?" he yelled into the phone. I slowly repeated what I said, tears falling freely. "Did you call the police?"

"No, not yet. I just got the news. She's probably long gone by now." I started crying harder.

"Honey, stop crying. Are the children okay?" Despite his concern, I detected the anger in his voice.

"Yes, they're fine."

"Amber, how do you know it was her?"

"When Kyra was describing the lady to me, I remember seeing that same person in the courtroom on Friday and then again today. She was dressed exactly the way Kyra described."

"Wait. Are you saying Sarah's stalking you again?"

"I believe so, Bryce."

"This is getting ridiculous! That lady is crazy!" I could tell he was beyond upset at that point. "Where are my children?"

"They're in their rooms."

"Put them on the phone, please. I want to talk to them." As each of the children spoke to their father, I listened as they recounted the events of the day. Kyra told him they would be glad when he came back home from his trip. "I should be home Saturday morning," he replied.

"In three days?" BJ shouted.

"Yes, son. In three days," he said happily before ending the call.

No sooner than that call disconnected, the phone rang again. It was my pastor's wife asking me to be the speaker at the women's luncheon on Saturday. "Okay. I will be there." I could hear the smile in her voice as we hung up the phone.

I then prepared dinner, thanking God that the lady didn't take my children. I said aloud, "Lord, thank You that my children didn't leave with that lady." My thoughts shifted to Olivia when I picked up a dish she had given me as a housewarming gift the first time she visited my house. I really miss her. She died not knowing Kyra was her children's half-sister. I prayed, "Lord, please watch over her children." After dinner, I played games with the children until it was time for them to go to bed.

Tuesday was a long day in court. After work, I stopped by Ms. Eva's to pick her up and the children, and we went to Applebee's for dinner. When I dropped Ms. Eva back at home, she said, "I really enjoyed dinner. Thanks for taking me out with you!"

I chuckled and said, "For all you do for us, it was payback."

On our ride home, I told Kyra and BJ that I was asked to speak at the women's luncheon on Saturday.

"What do I have to do?" Kyra asked.

"Just be there," I replied. "And BJ, all you have to do is sit, be quiet, and look handsome." That made him laugh. He chuckled all the way home.

Like clockwork, the phone was ringing when we entered the house. It was Bryce calling. "Where have you guys been?" he asked.

"We went out to dinner and took your mom with us."

"Nice! Where did you go?"

"To Applebee's."

He laughed and said, "When I get home, I'm taking you out to get some real food."

Both children wanted to talk to him, so I handed over the phone and went into the study to review my court case for the next day. Kyra called out to me and said, "Mama, daddy is ready to pray!" We gathered around the phone, turned on the speaker, and prayed.

After the prayer, Bryce said, "Babe, before you hang up... I should be home on Friday. The officer I was sitting in for came back today, so I will be leaving early Friday morning instead of Saturday."

"Okay! That's good. The Lord heard my prayers. I was asked to speak at the women's luncheon on Saturday at the church and need your support."

"If the Lord wills it, I will see you all on Friday," he replied before hanging up the phone.

Wednesday and Thursday passed quickly as I prepared for Saturday. On Friday morning, the children woke up early for school. They said they couldn't wait to get out so they could see their dad. In fact, they were up late Thursday night blowing up balloons, making a 'Welcome Home' sign, and baking a cake with "Welcome Home" on it. There were balloons everywhere!

As they stepped out the door to catch the bus, BJ exclaimed, "Mama, daddy is going to be surprised when he gets home!"

"Yes, he sure is!" I answered. I then got dressed and headed to work for the court hearing. I thought, *"Cases like the one I'm working on can get messy when they involve families and their children!"* As I passed by Olivia's house and saw the 'For Sale' sign in her yard, sadness overwhelmed me. I had to pray, knowing she was gone and I would never see her again.

During lunch break, I received a call from Bryce letting me know he was back in town. "Let the children stay at my mom's house. Three weeks is a long time to be without you, Babe," he teased.

"No can do, sir. They have a surprise waiting for you."

"It can't wait?" he asked, sounding disappointed.

"No, it can't."

"What is it?"

"Well, it wouldn't be a surprise if I told you, Bryce!"

He agreed and said, "I have a surprise for you and the children, too!" It was his turn to tease.

"What is it?"

"It won't be a surprise if I told you, Amber!" he replied, laughing. "I'll see you soon. I love you."

That afternoon, I picked up the children from Grandmom's house and headed home. It was after 4:30, and we were wondering what was taking Bryce so long to get home. Around 5:15, I heard him pull into the garage. I met him at the door and reminded him, "Be surprised, okay?" He nodded in agreement. I closed the door behind me and called out to the children, "Your daddy just pulled into the garage!"

They ran out of their bedroom, just as he opened the door. "Surprise!" they shouted.

"Wow! Did you guys do all this for me?" he asked, sounding genuinely surprised.

"Yes!" they shouted in unison.

I stood there, watching the children interact with their dad. I could tell by the look on his face that something was bothering him, but he still masked his unhappiness for the children. We had dinner, and the chatter was nonstop. The children had so much to talk about and tried to catch their dad up on all the events in one sitting. After dinner, Kyra brought in the "Welcome Home" cake from the kitchen.

"Oh, my goodness! That cake looks too good to cut, Kyra!" her daddy said happily.

"Cut it, dad!" Kyra said with a prideful smile.

He did as she requested, then took a bite of that slice. "Kyra, this is delicious! Are you sure you baked this cake? And where's the ice cream?" he teased.

"I'll get it!" she said, running into the kitchen. When she returned, she cut a slice of cake for the rest of us, adding a scoop of ice cream on the side.

The cake was really good! "Kyra, it is delicious, and the decoration is beautiful," I told her, complimenting her on her baking and decorating skills.

"Thank you, Mama!"

"Yes, your cake was perfect, Kyra. And Babe, I enjoyed the casserole, too," Bryce said.

After dinner, the children went to their rooms while Bryce and I cleaned up the kitchen. "What's on your mind, Hon?" I asked.

"Is it that obvious? Babe, I just want to hold you in my arms. It's been three long weeks since I last held you. I've missed you so much." He gave me a passionate kiss and suggested we take a shower together.

After the shower, I asked, "Now, can you tell me what's truly on your mind?"

He let out a long sigh. "Where do I start? I had a recruit come in to finish his enlistment papers. When I looked out the window, I saw this lady standing by his car. I assumed she was waiting for him. When he finished his paperwork and left, I watched as he got into his car, but the lady didn't get in. She was still there, walking back and forth. I opened the door and asked her if she was waiting for someone. She yelled back and said, 'I have been waiting to see you.' That's when I realized it was Sarah. She was wearing a black wig or had dyed her hair. She started screaming the same thing to me that she did in the mall. All the other officers came out of the building, staring at me. I was so embarrassed. I told her to leave, but she just kept getting louder, yelling, 'I want my son back!' I had to call the police to get her to quiet down. When the police arrived, one of them said that she had a mental health issue and that she had been taken into custody before. I then told them what she did to our

34

children and how she stalked you and came to your workplace. I also told them I believe she was the one who spray-painted my car." He paused to collect his thoughts and take a deep breath. "While telling the officers everything she had done, she blurted out, 'I went to that school to get my little boy!' They locked her in the backseat of a patrol car, which seemed to help calm her down. One of the officers explained that she had done something similar to another man, saying the man took his family and moved out of town. They asked me which days she was at the school and courthouse, then said they would check the cameras at both places to see if it was indeed her. If it is, she'll be gone for a long time." I guess because I wasn't reacting outwardly, Bryce paused and asked, "Are you asleep?"

"No. I'm just listening to and absorbing all that you're saying."

"Well, that's enough about Sarah," he said, pulling me close.

"Bryce, what if she had taken our children and we couldn't find them?" I asked with genuine concern.

"That's exactly why I pray for God's protection over our children every single day. I thank God they didn't go with her."

"I thank God, too," I said before getting up to go into the office to review my message for the women's luncheon. When I returned to the room, Bryce was sound asleep.

On Saturday morning, I woke up early, excited about the message and scriptures the Lord had given me. We ate breakfast and then left for the luncheon, which started at 11:30. Upon our arrival at the church, the parking lot was already packed. That's when the butterflies started fluttering in my stomach. I knew it was just the devil trying to instill fear, though. God had given me a powerful message to share in only ten minutes, along with two other women on the program who were scheduled to speak. By the time we entered, the program had already begun. After the general announcements, each speaker was called to deliver their message. I was the last to speak.

I stood behind the podium, praying that God would speak through me, and opened my Bible to the scripture God had given me: Jeremiah 29:11. From that passage, the Lord guided my words. I shared my testimony of how the Lord saved me. I told the audience there was a time when I was self-centered and thought I was all that and two bags of chips, not knowing I was on my way to Hell. I shared how my Mama prayed for me, and one night, she asked, "If the Lord comes back tonight, would you be ready to go back with Him?" I knew I didn't want to go to Hell, so I accepted the Lord that same night. "So, today, I'm asking each of you here the same question my Mama asked me: If the Lord comes today, will you be ready to go back with Him?" I then took my seat.

Five people gave their lives to the Lord that day.

After the luncheon, the pastor said to me, "The Lord gave me the same scripture for Sunday's message."

I smiled and replied, "By two or three witnesses, let every word be established."

He laughed and said, "The word you spoke was truly from the Lord because some of what you said is what He also gave me." His wife came over, hugged me, and said she enjoyed the service and my contribution.

As soon as we arrived home from church, Bryce surprised us with the gifts he had purchased for each of us. He gave Kyra a beautiful necklace and earring set featuring the letter 'K,' BJ received a new video game, and I got a gold chain with the children's birthstones set in a charm.

"Daddy, why didn't you give these to us yesterday? I could have worn mine to church today," Kyra mentioned while hugging him.

"Well, yesterday, you all surprised me. Today, I surprised you! BJ, your gift is for being quiet in church."

"I promise to always be quiet in church from now on," BJ replied in all seriousness. In response, Bryce rubbed him on his head, laughing.

Once in bed, Bryce said, "The Lord knew those people would give their lives to Him today. They needed to hear what you had to say. I enjoyed it, Babe." He sealed those words with a kiss goodnight.

****

In April, Bryce's sister and brother came into town from Montgomery, Alabama, to surprise their mom for her 64th birthday. His older brother's name is Allen, his wife's name is Megan, and they have three children: Allen Jr. (AJ), Hannah, and Denise. Allen Sr. was four years older than Bryce. His sister, Rachel, was married to John Harris, and they have two children:

fraternal boy and girl twins named Jessica and Jayson. Rachel was two years older than Bryce.

Bryce's task was to get his mom out of the house that Saturday morning and keep her busy until I arrived to set everything up at her place. He left early to take her out for breakfast, calling me shortly after to confirm they were gone and that the patio door was unlocked. When the children and I reached Ms. Eva's house, we unloaded the food from the car, and then I parked my SUV two houses down from her home. I then called Allen, who was waiting at the hotel for my call, to let him know their mom was out of the house. I asked him to stop by Romeo's to pick up the birthday cake, ribs, and chicken. Everything was paid for; he just needed to give them Bryce's name. I also told him to park at the 7-Eleven on the corner after we unloaded his car.

When Allen and Rachel arrived, Rachel helped me set up the food, and the younger girls took care of the decorating. "Who made all this food?" Rachel asked.

"Bryce and I did. If there's anything left, please take it home with you."

"I'm ready to eat now!" she joked, snacking on a chicken wing while we waited for Bryce and Ms. Eva to come back.

Around 11:30, Bryce called to let us know they were leaving the market and on their way home. When they got back, she walked through the front door, straight to the kitchen to wash her fresh fruits before putting them in the fruit bowl sitting on the kitchen table. Bryce sat at the table, talking to her while eating an apple. The rest of us came out of hiding, entered the kitchen, and yelled, "Happy Birthday!" She looked at us as if she had seen a ghost and began to cry.

"Sit down, Mama," Bryce said as he guided her to a chair.

"Where did all y'all come from?" The way she said it was so funny. "Baby Boy (that's what she called Bryce), did you know they were here?"

"Yes, ma'am. That's why I invited you to go out with me this morning!"

She smacked him on the arm. "Why didn't you tell me they were here?"

"Mama, if I told you, it wouldn't have been a surprise!" he said, laughing at the confused expression on her face.

"Baby Boy, you used to tell me everything."

Rachel was laughing as she added, "He sure did! He was a little spoiled brat who told on everything we did. He always got us in trouble with his tattletale ways. When he was around ten, he often came into my room uninvited. I would tell him to get out, but he wouldn't leave. One day, I pushed him out of my room and locked the door behind him. Just when I thought he was gone, he stuck his fingers under the door and said, 'I'm still in your room!' I threw one of my shoes, hitting his fingers, and he went and told Mama I hit him. I was grounded for that." Bryce was laughing so hard that tears rolled down his cheeks.

After we finished eating, Ms. Eva opened her gifts. My family gave her an Emeril Air Fryer. "Did Kyra tell you I wanted an air fryer?" she asked.

"Yes, ma'am. She did," I replied.

Rachel gave her a Victoria's Secret full-length plush robe and house shoes set, the girls gave her a Bath and Body Works gift set, and Allen gave her a ticket for a cruise. Ms. Eva was very grateful for her gifts and even asked her granddaughters if they wanted to go on the cruise with her next April. After the girls discussed it with their parents, they all received a 'yes' to go. "I'll have all my beautiful granddaughters on a cruise with me," she bragged, hugging them.

When it was time to leave, Bryce loaned his car to Rachel because she wanted to visit some friends while she was in town.

On the ride home, BJ asked, "Why does Kyra always get to go places, and I can't?"

"BJ, it's a Grandmom and granddaughter cruise this time," Bryce replied. BJ wasn't happy with that response at all. When we got home, it was after 10:30 p.m. Bryce called us all into the family room to pray before going to bed. Once we climbed into bed, he asked, "Babe, how are you feeling?"

"I'm feeling good, thinking about how happy your mom was to see you all there. It made me think of my mom."

"You know, Allen and Rachel thought I got away with a lot because I was the youngest, but they would be wrong," he said, gently changing the subject.

"I bet you were a naughty little brat, though."

He nodded and laughed, saying, "I did tell on them, especially when Rachel had boys in the house when Mama wasn't home. She would be so angry at me when I told on her."

"I guess now, you can see why Kyra is always angry at BJ. He's always telling on her about something," I replied with a giggle.

He began placing gentle kisses on my face and said, "That's what boys do. They tell everything."

On Sunday morning, our family went to Sunday school. When the service was about to start, Allen, Rachel, and their families arrived with Ms. Eva. I could see their Mama was happy to have all her children in church with her. After church, we all went to Ms. Eva's house and ate the leftover food from her party. We stayed there until Allen, Rachel, and their families left to go back to Alabama.

Shortly after they left, Bryce hugged his mom and headed out with BJ. Kyra and I stayed behind to help Ms. Eva tidy up and put everything back in place. When we finished, we hugged her goodbye and went home. By the time we got there, Bryce and BJ were already in bed. I said goodnight to Kyra, and she went into her room. I quickly showered and then got into bed, cuddling up close to Bryce.

"Amber, do you want to have a baby?" he asked unexpectedly.

"I thought you were asleep, Hon. What made you think about a baby?"

"I was just lying here thinking. In three years, Kyra will go off to college, and BJ will be 13. What are we going to do with ourselves?"

"You know, a baby sounds good to me," was my honest answer.

We tried to get pregnant for over eight months after that conversation, but our efforts didn't result in pregnancy. One night, while lying in bed, Bryce suggested we take a romantic vacation to relax, and he said he would ask his mother to watch the children.

Around 4:30 the next morning, we were awakened by a call from my Mama. She was crying, saying that my Aunt Edna had been rushed to the hospital, and the prognosis didn't look good for her. After hanging up, I thought about the time Mama visited Aunt Edna and Uncle Otis 11 years ago in Virginia. At that time, they asked her to move in with them, but she told them she didn't want to leave me in Dallas alone, so she came back to live with me after selling her house. When she saw this house, she fell in love with it immediately. "Amber, call the realtor back right now. We must buy this house. I have the down payment for it. And I want the two bedrooms in the back of the house with my own bathroom," she said urgently.

I remember how excited Mama was to move in. After six months of Mama living with me, she got a call from Aunt Edna, saying Uncle Otis was in the hospital. She immediately left to help them, but two weeks later, Uncle Otis died. After the funeral, Aunt Edna wanted Mama to stay with her since they were both widows, so she did. Now, Aunt Edna isn't doing well, and Mama wants me to be with her. I didn't know what to do.

At breakfast, I talked it over with Bryce. He told me to go be with Mama and said he would keep the children at home so they wouldn't need to be pulled from school. "When you get back, we will go on our getaway," he said before kissing me and leaving for work.

I flew out of Dallas that Friday morning and arrived in Hampton, Virginia, around noon. I rented a car and drove to Aunt Edna's house. When I got there, Mama was pulling into the garage. As she got out of the car, she was crying. I walked up to her and held her as she said, "I'm glad you're here. Edna left me at 10:15 this morning." Mama was utterly devastated and cried nearly all afternoon.

I called Bryce to share the news. He was sorry to hear about my aunt and said he'd fly out to be with me and let his Mama watch the children. I told him not to come because we needed to handle the funeral arrangements, and since she just died, I didn't know when the funeral would be. He understood and called to check on Mama and me every night, and let me talk to the children.

Five days into my stay in Virginia, I woke up feeling unusually nauseous. I started thinking I might be pregnant after all, but I refused to mention it to Bryce until I was sure.

Early Friday morning, on the day of the funeral, I received a call from Bryce, asking for the address of my aunt's house. "Are you in Virginia?" I asked, surprised.

"Yes, I am. Please give me the address." When he arrived, he had the children with him. I was so happy to see them. Mama was glad they were there, too.

During the funeral service, Mama struggled to deal with her loss. I was glad Bryce was there to help me with her.

On Sunday morning, Bryce and the children flew back to Dallas. I stayed for a week, helping Mama with paperwork and anything else she needed. When it was time for me to return to Dallas, I asked her to come with me. That's when she told me that after Uncle Otis died, Aunt Edna changed her will and left everything to her: a four-bedroom house, two cars, two rental properties, and a large sum of money. Mama did say she would stay with me for a couple of weeks while she figured out what to do next.

We flew out Saturday afternoon. When we got home, she walked into her bedroom at my house and said, "This is beautiful. You decorated my room with butterflies." She stood there for a moment, looking around, before saying, "Amber, I can't believe you fixed this up for me."

"Yes, Mama. I knew you'd come back one day. Remember, this is what you paid for. Now, I didn't knock out that wall over there yet."

She laughed and replied, "I really liked this house for you and me, Kyra." Mama enjoyed herself in her small apartment at the back of the house. She cooked for us every day. We hardly saw the children during her visit. Around the two-week mark, I knew she would soon have to head back to Virginia. During her stay, her friends kept calling, asking when she was coming back. I could tell she missed her friends. After three weeks, she returned to her inheritance left by Aunt Edna. I dropped her off at the airport and cried as I watched her plane take off.

On my way home from the airport, I stopped at Rite Aid to buy a pregnancy test. When I got home, I took the test, and it was positive! I couldn't wait for Bryce to get home! At 4:00 p.m., he drove into the garage. I met him at the door in my birthday suit. "Oh, my God! Amber! Where are the children?" He looked around frantically.

I laughed so hard and replied, "They are at your Mama's house. Hon, we are pregnant!" He grabbed me, pulled me close, and kissed me all over my face. I couldn't stop laughing at his level of excitement. We decided not to tell the children and our mothers until after our first visit to the doctor. That Friday afternoon, we left the children with Ms. Eva and drove to New Orleans for our romantic weekend getaway.

A couple of weeks later, Bryce came home from work and said, "The police stopped by the office to look at the security camera footage. They saw the person near my car but couldn't identify the face. However, the cameras at the school and courthouse confirmed the woman was Sarah. The officer said they spoke with Sarah's sister. It turns out Sarah was in a car accident where her boyfriend and young son were killed instantly. After the accident, she had a nervous breakdown and has never fully recovered."

The latter part of Bryce's report broke my heart. "I'm sure the loss of her child and boyfriend was hard on her," I replied.

We prayed for Sarah that night. Afterward, Bryce asked, "Did you make an appointment to see the doctor?"

"Yes. It's next Tuesday at 2:00 p.m."

"Okay. I'll leave work early and meet you there."

On Monday, I had parent-teacher conferences with the children's teachers. Both Kyra and BJ were doing well in their classes. Bryce told them they would get $10.00 for every 'A,' $5.00 for every 'B,' and nothing for 'Cs.' I smiled as I left, thinking he's going to be out $60.00 for Kyra and $40.00 for BJ.

That afternoon, when the children arrived home from school, they were excited to learn about their grades and how much money their father owed them. Soon after, we heard Bryce drive into the garage. When he entered the house, Kyra and BJ bombarded him, telling him all about their grades. "Wait a minute, kids! May I at least get a kiss from my wife?" he joked as he kissed me. "Now, let me see your report cards." He glanced over each one and said, "Wow! You're doing great in your classes! That's a lot of money I owe you. I'll have to give you an I.O.U. until the weekend, though. You're draining my pockets with these good grades and sending me to the poor house," he joked as he hugged them.

"Okay, you guys. Dinner is ready. Go and wash your hands," I interjected. I really hated having to disrupt their good time.

After dinner, we began Bible study at 6:00. It was interesting to hear the questions the children asked about life and everything else their curious minds wanted to explore. I was glad, knowing we had the scriptures to provide us with the answers. After Bible study, we prayed, and then the children went to their rooms to wind down for the night.

When Tuesday afternoon came, Bryce met me at the doctor's office as planned. The doctor said I was doing well and that I was 16 weeks pregnant. I asked Bryce, "Now that it's confirmed, when are we going to tell the children about the baby?"

"I have to head back to the office now, but I'll be home around 5:00. We'll tell them together." He kissed me, and we parted ways.

On the way home, I picked up pizza for dinner. As I pulled up to the house, I immediately noticed the garage door was open. That's when I remembered the children had a half-day, but they knew they were never supposed to leave the garage door open. I stood in the doorway of the kitchen, observing them. They were so engrossed in conversation in the family room that they didn't even hear me come in, so I listened to them talk.

Kyra: "BJ, if you don't tell, I'll give you $5.00."

BJ: "When daddy pays us, I'll have my own money."

Kyra: "I'll let you come into my room anytime you want."

BJ: "I don't want to come into your room!"

I thought, *"What in the world has Kyra done that she doesn't want BJ to tell?"* I intentionally made some noise in the kitchen, and both of them came running, stopping at the island. "Why did you guys leave the garage door open? If your dad arrived before me, both of you would've been in big trouble." Kyra looked at BJ nervously.

"Kyra was the last one to come in. She told me to go into the house. And Mama, Kyra was in the..." BJ said.

Kyra cut him off and said, "Mama, I see you got pizza. Can we eat now?"

"No, not until your daddy gets here. Kyra, I want you and BJ to change the sheets on your beds and put the dirty ones in the washing machine."

"Do you want me to put my sheets with Kyra's?" BJ asked.

"Yes, and grab clean ones from the shelf in your closet to put on your beds," I instructed. As they walked away, I heard Kyra whisper something to BJ. What in the world had she done that she doesn't want BJ to tell?

Around 4:30, Bryce came home. No sooner than he walked into the kitchen, BJ came running and said, "Daddy, when are you going to pay me for my grades?"

"May I get settled before you start asking about that money?" He sat on the couch, and BJ plopped down next to him.

"Tomorrow, we are having a pop-up store at school, and I need my money so I can buy something," BJ explained.

"Okay, BJ. I hear you. Where is Mama?"

"She's in the laundry room, folding clothes."

Just then, Kyra walked in. "Hi, daddy!"

"Hello, Kyra. How was your day at school, guys?"

"Good," she replied, hugging him.

"I did well in school today, too. We had a half-day," BJ announced.

I stood quietly in the doorway of the laundry room, waiting to see if BJ would tell their father about Kyra. I could see Kyra nervously looking at BJ.

"Daddy, Kyra had a boy in the garage." There it was. BJ tattletaled. Bryce sat straight up on the couch at the news.

I walked into the family room and asked, "Kyra, you had a boy in the garage?"

Before she could answer, BJ continued, "Yes, and she told me to go into the house." He looked at Kyra, moving his head from side to side, and said, "See? I told you I was going to tell!"

She looked at BJ angrily with tears in her eyes. "I wasn't out there for a long time," she explained before turning to go to her bedroom.

"Dad, maybe you should take her phone away. She's on it all the time, talking and talking," BJ suggested.

"BJ, let me deal with this," Bryce said sternly. "Go into your room and do your homework."

"I already did my homework."

I asked, "Did you put the clean sheets on your bed yet?"

"Oh. No. I forgot," he said, getting up and rushing away. We heard Kyra call him a blabbermouth as he ran past her room. "I told you I was going to tell."

"Shut up. Don't talk to me. You talk too much. Get away from me!" she spat.

"Bryce, what are you going to do about this?" I asked, my question laden with worry.

"I'll talk to her. Just let me rest my mind for a minute," he replied, gently pulling me onto the couch beside him. "Babe, don't worry. I have everything on camera."

"Camera? Where do you have a camera?"

"Let me show you. We'll see how truthful Kyra is." He pulled out his phone, and he opened the app to show the replay of Kyra's time in the garage. "See? If anyone approaches the house, I can see. I had already told both of them that I don't want anyone here when we aren't home, but while you were in Virginia, BJ had his little friend lying on the couch, playing his game, and eating a sandwich. Plus, there's the situation with Sarah. One day, she left an envelope in our mailbox."

"She was here? At our house? What was in the envelope?" I asked, alarmed.

"A picture of me when I was running track and a note that read, 'I'm sorry. Have a nice life. Sarah.' That incident prompted me to install an outdoor camera. I talked to Ed, the policeman down the street. He documented everything and said he'd keep a lookout for us."

"Where is the picture? I want to see it."

"It's on the table. I look like an 18-year-old BJ," he said, laughing. "I saw you on camera carrying a pizza. I'm hungry."

"I'll get it out of the oven so we can eat and tell the children we're pregnant."

"Let's not tell them yet. We'll get through this issue with Kyra first and then tell them tomorrow," Bryce suggested while rubbing my belly.

As we gathered around the table to eat dinner, Kyra shot an angry look at BJ, but he seemed unfazed. After Bryce blessed the food, the first thing out of BJ's mouth was, "Daddy, what are you going to do about Kyra having that boy in the garage?"

"You just want me to get in trouble!" Kyra yelled across the table.

"Lower your voice around the dinner table, young lady," I stated firmly.

"BJ is just trying to get me in trouble, and I didn't do anything," she whined.

"Okay, Kyra. Tell me why you had a boy at this house when I warned you not to have anyone here when your Mama and I aren't home," Bryce demanded.

"Daddy, we just stood in the garage and talked. His name is Jessie, and he lives in the next subdivision. He didn't come inside the house. That's just BJ blowing stuff all out of control."

"Oh. Alright. As long as he wasn't inside the house, that's okay," Bryce said with a smile.

Kyra burst out laughing. "See? You had my heart beating fast for nothing." We all laughed at her reaction.

After dinner, Bryce told them that he could see them on his phone both inside and outside the house, but he didn't specify where the cameras were located. They looked all around, trying to find them. "Dad, where are they? I just want to see what they look like," Kyra said.

He laughed. "You think you're slick. I'm not going to tell you!"

She then looked at me. "Mama, do you know where they are?"

"Yes, I do, but I'm not telling you either."

"Both of you are wrong for that!" she said with a chuckle on her way to her room.

On Friday, after Bryce got home from work, we all went out to dinner at Cracker Barrel. Bryce told them they could order whatever they wanted to eat and gave them their money for their good grades. "Do we have to pay for our own dinner?" BJ asked.

"Yes, sir! If you want to eat, you will!" Bryce stated.

We gave the waitress our order but had to wait for BJ to decide. Finally, he said, "I want a hamburger, French fries, and a cookie." Bryce made sure to tell the waitress that the children were paying for their own meals.

Once the food was brought to our table, Kyra said, "BJ, that's all you ever order. You're going to be hungry once we leave here."

"I can eat more when I get home. I don't want to spend all my money on this food," he replied.

While we ate, Bryce shared the news about the baby. Kyra was thrilled! "Is that the reason you want us to pay for our dinner? Because you're having a baby?" BJ asked.

"No. I'm not paying for your dinner because you have your own money," Bryce reminded him. All of us burst out laughing.

After getting home, we prayed and went to bed. Around 10:30, we heard someone in the kitchen. Bryce called out, "Who's that in the kitchen?"

"It's me, dad," BJ answered.

"What are you doing in there?"

"I'm making some ramen noodles and a peanut butter and jelly sandwich. I'm hungry!" Bryce and I laughed until tears streamed down our faces.

About a month later, as we were watching TV in bed, there was a knock at our bedroom door. "Who is it?" I called out.

"Kyra."

"Come in." She got into the bed, crawling between Bryce and me. "What are you doing, girl?"

"I'm lying here between my two favorite people, whom I love very much," she said with a cheesy smile.

"Oh, no. What did you break?" Bryce asked curiously.

"Daddy, I haven't broken anything!"

"Well, why are you in our bed?" He and I waited patiently for her response.

"Please don't say no, but can I go to Bay City?"

"What? Who do you know that lives in Bay City?" he asked.

"Zoe and Carlos live in Bay City now, and Carlos said there's an amusement park called Cedar Point in Sandusky, Ohio. He said it's the biggest amusement park in the world and that they are going in July. Can I go with them? Daddy, say yes, please!"

Bryce sat up in bed. "Kyra, who is Carlos?"

"My other brother," she stated matter-of-factly. "Remember, they stayed down the street, and their mother died?"

I joined the conversation. "Wait, Kyra. You still talk to them?"

"Yes, I talk to them all the time!"

"Wow. I didn't know that," I replied, curious about what their conversations entailed.

"Yep! I talk to Zoe and their daddy, too."

My heart started to race. "When did all this start?"

"Mama, I've been talking to them since they left. Their daddy got married to a lady named Lorie. Zoe said she is good to them and that they can do whatever they want. When I talked to their daddy, he said he wants to see me and would like me to come visit them sometime."

I felt anger rising within me. "Oh, he did? Why would he want you to come and visit him? He doesn't even know you."

"I don't know, but that's what he said. And Zoe said they're going to Alabama in August and that Lorie is going, too." I remained quiet as she talked about Zoe, Carlos, and their daddy. Bryce hadn't said anything more one way or another. "Daddy, are you asleep?"

"No, I'm awake."

"Well, what do you think about me going to Michigan?"

"Kyra, you'll have to ask your Mama about that." I acted like I had fallen asleep.

"She'll just say, 'Whatever your father says is alright with me.'"

"I don't know what she'll say, though, Kyra. She's asleep now. I guess we'll talk about this another time."

"Okay, daddy. Goodnight," she said as she climbed out of the bed and closed the door behind her.

"Don't forget to say your prayers!" Bryce yelled.

"I know, dad!" she yelled back.

A few days later, Bryce seemed bothered. "I've noticed Kyra hasn't spoken to me in the last few days. She comes home, goes straight to her room, and stays there unless one of us calls for her. She hasn't said anything to me since she asked about going to Bay City."

"She'll be okay, Hon. She needs to realize she can't always get what she wants."

Two more weeks pass. On a Thursday, as I was leaving work, Bryce called and said, "I'm feeling bad about the way Kyra is acting toward me, but I don't think she should go to Bay City. She doesn't know those people. She's my little girl, and my job is to protect her. After all, that man hasn't called or said anything whatsoever to us about her."

"Bryce, whatever decision you make, I will support."

"That's exactly what Kyra said you would say," he replied, laughing.

"Hon, stop worrying. She'll be okay. You're the one who's spoiling the mess out of her anyway. Notice she doesn't try that stuff with me."

He couldn't stop laughing. "How are you feeling, Babe?"

"I'm feeling pretty good today."

"Great! I'll see you soon. Be careful out there. I love you."

When I made it home, the children were in their rooms. I called out and asked, "What are you guys doing?"

BJ yelled, "I'm doing my homework, and Kyra is asleep."

"Wake her up and come here."

When Kyra walked into the family room, she hugged me and said, "Sorry, Mama. I was asleep. We had gym today, and I'm tired."

"Well, your father said you should be ready to go when he gets here."

"Where are we going?" she asked.

"I don't know. He didn't tell me."

"Can I go?" BJ asked.

"No. I'm sorry. This is daddy-daughter bonding time."

"When are we going to have Mama-son bonding time?"

"We'll go for a walk through the mall. How's that?" I replied enthusiastically.

"Let me put on my shoes!" he said excitedly, heading to his bedroom.

When Bryce came home, he handed me six long-stem roses and planted a sweet kiss on my lips before calling out to Kyra, "Are you ready for our date?"

"Yes, I am! Where are we going?" I heard her ask as they walked out the door.

BJ called out from behind me, "I'm ready!" As promised, we took a walk in the mall and grabbed a bite to eat at Chick-fil-A. We were already home by the time Bryce and Kyra came back.

"Mama, I'm going to model the new clothes daddy bought me," Kyra said happily.

"Okay. I will be waiting!"

Bryce walked in and asked, "Babe, how are you feeling?" as he rubbed my growing belly.

"I'm fine. Where did you go on your date?"

"We actually went somewhere I said I would never go with Kyra without you: to the mall. I told her to pick two outfits.

That girl took almost two hours to find two outfits! One hour at Justice, and another hour at 5,7,9." We were cracking up as he told me about their adventures.

After a short while, Kyra came in wearing her first new outfit. "How do you like it, Mama?"

"That's really cute, Kyra! It looks very nice on you."

"Wait until you see the next one!" she exclaimed, leaving to change.

"So, how did your talk with her go?" I asked Bryce.

"It went well. After we finished shopping, we stopped to eat at the food court. Of course, she talked about going to Bay City and said she was disappointed that we wouldn't let her go. I explained to her that Zoe's father hadn't called to speak with either of us, and that I was upset about him making all these promises to her. I told her maybe one summer we will all take a family trip to Cedar Point, but right now, it isn't a good idea for her to go alone. After that, she talked a lot about Zoe and Carlos."

Just then, Kyra walked in, wearing her second outfit. This time, she had her hair down with a matching headband. "Mama, how do you like this one?"

"I like that one, too, and those shoes will look good with both outfits!"

Bryce laughed and said, "You look too grown-up in that one."

"Daddy, remember: I'm almost 14!"

"Yes, I know. That's why you might need to take that one back!"

She knew he was joking. "Haha, daddy! Thank you so much. I love my new outfits!"

"As you should! It took you long enough to find them!"

Kyra kissed us both before saying goodnight, adding, "I won't forget to pray, daddy."

"Oh, my goodness. My little girl is growing up," Bryce said with a sigh.

That night, Bryce had trouble sleeping. He got up early at 6:30, getting ready for work. As he prepared to leave, he said, "I'll call you when I get to work."

"Wait, Hon. Why were you tossing and turning in your sleep last night? Are you okay?"

"I have a mild headache, but I took a Tylenol. I'll be fine."

"I'm going to be in a preliminary hearing all day today. I'll call you during my lunch break to check on you."

"Okay. Thank you, Babe."

Later that morning, while I was doing my devotion, Kyra came into my room complaining about her head and stomach hurting. "Is it time for your cycle?" I asked.

"No, I already had it," she answered.

"Look in the medicine cabinet and take a teaspoon of that Pepto-Bismol." After taking the medicine, she went back to her room. About ten minutes later, she ran back into my room, saying she had to vomit. "Go into my bathroom! Hurry!" As soon as she entered, I heard her vomiting. I followed her in and asked, "Are you alright now?" She nodded yes. I then laid my hand on her head, prayed, and told her, "Go lie down. Don't go to school today. I'll tell BJ to stay home with you."

I got dressed for work. Before leaving, I peeked in on Kyra, who was still asleep. Once I arrived at work, I called the school to let them know the kids wouldn't be in class that day. I tried calling Bryce to tell him the children were home, but he didn't answer, so I left a message. During my lunch break, I called home to check on Kyra. She said she felt better when she woke up and that she would have dinner ready for us. She also mentioned making her daddy one of her tasty cakes again. "Okay. Be careful in the kitchen. I gotta go. I love you." I thought, *"That girl loves to cook and bake. She gets that from Ms. Eva."*

I then called Bryce's phone, but he still didn't answer. I looked at my texts and saw a message from Ms. Eva that read: "At emergency with Bryce." Oh, my God! She texted at 10:15 this morning! Emergency? Lord, what's wrong with my husband? I tried to call Ms. Eva but didn't get an answer. I had to tell myself to calm down. I called the first hospital that came to mind, Parkland, and asked if they had a patient there by the name of Bryce Hollinger.

"Yes," the woman said. "He's in room 345, third floor."

"Thank you," I replied, hanging up the phone. One of the assistants knocked on my door and said the judge was back. I walked into the courtroom on shaky legs, praying my husband was okay. Unfortunately, the hearing seemed to drag on endlessly. The other lawyer asked numerous questions, keeping the witness on the stand for quite some time. I could tell the jurors were getting restless as well. By the end of the hearing, we still weren't ready for the verdict. The judge scheduled another day for us to return.

I left immediately and went to the hospital to be by my husband's side. His mother was there, sitting by his bed and reading the Bible. He was asleep. I hugged her and asked what happened. "He had the worst case of food poisoning," she replied.

"Food poisoning? What did he eat?" I couldn't even imagine where he might have eaten something that put him in the hospital.

"He told the nurse the last thing he ate was a Reuben sandwich with sauerkraut at the food court in the mall."

"Ms. Eva, Kyra got up this morning complaining about her stomach. Both of them ate together while at the mall yesterday. After taking a dose of Pepto-Bismol, she vomited. I had her stay home from school today, with BJ watching over her. When I called home a little while ago, she was up and feeling better. Thank God.

"Well, it was so bad, they had to pump Bryce's stomach," she said.

As we talked, Bryce woke up. "What are you two talking about?"

"You, Hon. How are you feeling?" I inquired with concern.

"Better than I did when I came in here. That Reuben sandwich did a job on me." I then told him about Kyra not feeling well. "Oh, no. Is she alright?" he asked.

"Yes, she's okay now."

He chuckled and said, "She ate some of my sandwich. Once she took a bite, she said she didn't like it, so she ate her chicken sandwich and fries. They're going to keep me here overnight. You ladies go home. Please take my mom to my job to get my car." We prayed together before leaving, and Bryce fell back to sleep.

I took Ms. Eva to pick up Bryce's car, and she followed me home. When we walked in without Bryce, Kyra asked, "Where is daddy?"

"He's in the hospital. The food he ate yesterday at the food court made him sick," I told them. BJ started crying. "He's okay, BJ. They just want to keep him overnight."

"Grandmom, I made baked spaghetti and a cake. Are you staying with us tonight?" Kyra asked.

"No, baby girl. Your mom is going to take me home. I drove your dad's car here."

"Do you want me to make you a plate to go?"

"Yes, I'd like that. And don't forget a slice of your cake, too!"

The children rode with me to drop off Ms. Eva. When we got back home, we ate the dinner Kyra had made for us.

Everything was tasty! I especially enjoyed her baked spaghetti, garlic bread, and tossed salad. "Kyra, you're a good cook!"

"Thanks, Mama. Save room for the cake. It's coconut with cream cheese icing."

"Wonderful! And Kyra, since you cooked, I'll clean the kitchen." After nibbling on a small piece of cake, it was time for the children to get ready for bed. "Goodnight, you two. Thank you, Kyra, for the delicious dinner." Just as I finished cleaning up, the phone rang. It was Ms. Eva. "Hello?"

"Hi, Amber. Is Kyra still awake?"

"I think so."

"I want to tell her how much I enjoyed the food she made. That cake was delicious!"

I chuckled. "Yes, it was. Even BJ enjoyed it, and you know how picky that boy is." I called out for Kyra to pick up the phone and then hung up my side so she and her Grandma could talk. As I put away the last of the dishes, my cell phone rang. It was Bryce calling.

"Hi, Babe. Why is the house phone line busy?"

"Your mom and Kyra got a conversation going about how good the meal was that Kyra cooked for us."

"Really? What did she make this time?" he asked, sounding a little jealous. I told him about the tasty dinner and dessert, to which he replied, "Hey! You guys weren't supposed to cut my cake without me there!" His laughter was contagious.

"You know, while we were at the mall, she told me she wanted to go to culinary baking school.

"Wow. When we were driving to get your car, your mom told me she is praying that God blesses her with a building."

Bryce laughed and said, "Oh, so those two are planning on going into business together? Kyra told me the bakery's name will be 'E and K Bakery and Sandwich Shop.' I miss you, Babe."

"You went to sleep on us when we were there."

"Blame it on the medication they gave me."

"What time will they release you tomorrow?" I asked.

"I'm not sure, but I'll call Mama to pick me up. I know you'll be in court. Amber, I've been lying here, thinking about how precious life is. Ending up in the hospital wasn't part of my plan for the day. We never know when death will come knocking, so we need to live every day as if it's our last while pleasing God. In Jeremiah, it says, 'Blessed is the man who believes in, trusts in, and relies on the Lord.' I kept repeating in my mind, *'Lord, I believe in You.'* That scripture from Jeremiah came to me when I felt I was about to die, but I knew it was the Lord who kept me. These days, people are trying so hard to live long but not preparing to die."

"Why are you talking like that, Bryce? The Lord has blessed you, and you're recovering well." We talked until it was time for me to shower and go to bed. Before hanging up, we prayed together.

The next morning, the children and I overslept, so I had to rush them to school. I made it to work just in time to lock up my purse and get into the courtroom. Thank God, the jurors reached a verdict, and I won the case. By the time I got home that afternoon, Bryce had come from the hospital and even trimmed the trees in the front yard. When I got out of the car, he walked over and gave me a long hug. "You are so beautiful. I missed lying beside you last night," he said.

"I missed you, too. Where are the children?"

"In the house somewhere, trying to hide from doing some work," he joked. "When Mama brought me home, she and Kyra cooked dinner. I could smell fried chicken, but I don't know what else."

When Bryce and I went inside the house, Kyra said, "You guys wash your hands. Dinner is ready." We sat at the table, eating and chatting until late afternoon.

Bryce was off from work Thursday and Friday. When I got home from work on Thursday, I immediately noticed he had installed a fence along the backyard. On Friday morning, he took the children to an awards program at school, and that afternoon, he helped his Mama clean out her garage.

Monday was Memorial Day. After breakfast, we all went to the cemetery to visit our fathers' graves before attending a cookout at Ms. Eva's house. While we were there, his brother called to FaceTime them. He mentioned there would be a family reunion in August, from the 11th to the 13th, in New Hope, Alabama, and they asked each family to pay $150.00. That price included the cost of T-shirts for all of us, food for the picnic, and dinner.

"That's ironic. I will be on a job assignment there that same week," Bryce stated.

Ms. Ava asked, "Allen, do you think I can take my cruise then?"

"Mama, I thought you said you wanted to go on your birthday next April."

"Yes, I did say that, but I'm getting older, and people are dying around here! I think I need to go on my cruise before it's too late." Allen and Bryce laughed so hard at how serious she was.

"Mama, you'll be here a long time," Bryce said assuredly.

"Still, it's a good idea," Allen interjected. "If that's what you want to do, we can arrange for you to leave the same week Bryce will be here. Rachel or I can get you to the cruise ship in Mobile."

"Remember, the girls are coming with me," she replied.

Allen said, "All that will be taken care of when you get here."

"I'll CashApp you the money for Kyra's ticket along with the reunion money," Bryce added.

"No, bro. You don't have to send any money for her. I'll get her ticket. I get discounts. I'm a cruise ship coordinator, remember?" he said, laughing.

"Okay, big bro! Thank you!" Bryce said before ending the call. "We have to get ready to go. Where is Kyra?"

"She's asleep in the living room," BJ answered, turning to go get her.

"Don't wake her," Ms. Eva said. "She's not feeling well. Just let her sleep. She can catch the bus from here."

"Amber, we are making plans. Will you be okay to travel?" Bryce asked me.

"Yes, I should be able to go. I'll be okay."

Ms. Eva was observing our conversation closely. "What's this about, questioning whether you can travel?"

"I'm pregnant, Ms. Eva. Bryce didn't tell you?"

She sat up straight in a flash. "No, he didn't!"

"Yes, I did, Mama. I told you when I was helping you clean out the garage!"

"I don't remember you telling me anything like that! I'd remember!"

"I told you that Amber had a bun in the oven."

She slapped him on the arm and said, "Boy, I thought you were talking about some bread!"

We laughed hysterically as we walked out the door. "Thank you for the cookout, Ms. Eva!" I said appreciatively.

Bryce called for BJ to hurry up. I could tell he didn't want to leave with us because he was walking slowly. On our way home, BJ commented, "Now, I'll have to get on the bus by myself."

Bryce told him, "You won't be the only one out there getting on that bus."

The following morning, Bryce kissed me on my forehead before leaving for work and then called out to BJ to get up. I heard BJ reply that he was already awake and asked if Kyra would be on the bus. "Yes, she will be on the bus. You know the bus stops at the store by Grandmama's house."

"Why did she have to stay at Grandmama's house anyway?" BJ whined.

"Because Grandmama wanted her to stay. That's why. Get ready for school," Bryce stated as he headed out the door.

A few minutes later, BJ knocked on my bedroom door. "Enter," I said.

"Mama, I've been up for a long time," he stated sadly.

"Why did you get up so early? And you're dressed already?"

"Kyra always wakes me up, but she's not here, so I woke up by myself." Since he was wide awake, he stayed in my room for a while, and we discussed school and other topics. A bit later, I told him to look out and see if any children were standing at the bus stop. He left the room, came back, hugged me, and said, "I see my friend Joel out there. Bye, Mama!" I wondered, *"What is he going to do when Kyra graduates in a couple of years?"*

When BJ left the house, I got dressed and went into the kitchen to make myself some breakfast. From where I sat, I looked out the window and saw the children boarding the bus.

Ms. Eva called to let me know Kyra was waiting at the bus stop near her house. "Thanks for letting me know. BJ will be happy to see her."

She started laughing and said, "He called her twice last night, and this morning, he called to wake her up." That report made me laugh. BJ seemed to leave that part out of our morning discussion.

"Okay, Ms. Eva. I have to run now so I can get to work on time. We'll talk this afternoon."

"Okay. Bye-bye," she said, ending the call.

On my way to work, I remembered that Friday was Mama's 59th birthday. I made a mental note to get her a card and to tell her I was pregnant. Later that afternoon, I stopped at Bath and Body Works and picked out a complete toiletry set for her, placed one of the baby's ultrasound images in the box along with a birthday card, and dropped it off at the post office before it closed to mail it to her. I knew she would be surprised when she received it.

Friday was a short day at work. I picked up the children from Ms. Eva's, and we went to their school to get their class schedule for the upcoming school year. Kyra was entering 10th grade, and BJ would be starting 6th grade. I then called Bryce at work and told him to meet us at Golden Corral for dinner.

When we got home after dinner, we played games with the children before they went to their rooms for the night. Bryce went into the bedroom to watch TV, and I went into Mama's room to FaceTime her for her birthday. Before I could call her, she called me, excitedly saying how much she loved her gift. She opened the card while we were on the call, read it, and yelled, "Amber, you're pregnant?"

"Yes, ma'am! I am!"

"When is the baby due?"

"In October."

"I want to be there!"

"Mama, I would love for you to be here."

"I can see you're in my room," she said, laughing.

"Yes. I wanted to be in your room when I wished you a happy birthday!"

"Look in the top dresser drawer, Amber. I have something in there for you."

"Mama, it's your birthday, not mine!" I said, getting up to look in the drawer.

"Do you see the book I made for you?" she asked.

"Yes, Mama. It's beautiful."

"Open it. It's a book about our family."

"Mama, you wrote this about you and daddy?"

"Yes. The first page is about the first house we lived in. Your daddy and I were married five years before he went into the Army. Brandon was going on five, and you were two. Your daddy loved his little Amber Rose, and Brandon was a spitting image of him. He was the one who named you. I chose your middle name."

When she paused to take a breath, I asked, "Mama, why is there a cassette and a box in this plastic bag?"

She let out a gentle sigh. "Your father mailed it to me, saying that was how we would communicate with each other. He wanted to hear our voices while he was away, and he would talk on it and return it, letting me know what was happening over there." I could see the smile on her face when she talked about him. As she spoke, tears welled up in her eyes. "I received that cassette tape three weeks after his memorial service, along with that box containing a locket. Inside the locket is a picture of you and me, and one of Brandon and him. I didn't want to hear his voice again so soon after his passing, so I put it away for safekeeping."

"Mama, do you want me to play the cassette so you can hear what's on it?"

She hesitated before responding. "Okay. We can listen to it together. I wish Brandon were here to hear it with us." I placed the phone on the dresser and hurried to get the cassette player from my office. When I returned, Mama said, "It's been over 25 years since I heard his voice." As soon as I put the tape into the player, her doorbell rang. "Amber, that's the ladies from the center coming to take me out for dinner and a movie. We'll listen to the tape another day. I gotta go now."

"Okay, Mama. I love you. Enjoy your dinner and movie!" I then placed the cassette back in the plastic bag and flipped through the pictures in the book. Bryce called my phone, asking where I was. "I'm in Mama's room."

When he walked in, he asked, "What are you doing back here?"

"I was FaceTiming Mama for her birthday. She told me to look in the drawer and get this book. This is my family book." I pointed at each picture, telling him who they were and sharing what Mama had told me.

"This lady looks like you," Bryce observed.

"That's my grandmother. Mama's mother. This is my brother Brandon. He's two years older than I am and works as an FBI Secret Service Agent."

"Wow! That's impressive!"

"Are the children asleep yet?"

"Yes, I checked on them before coming back here." I told him I'd like to sleep in Mama's bed that night. He rubbed my belly and said, "If you sleep in here, I'm going to sleep in here, too." When I woke up the next morning, he had already left for work. Kyra found me and asked why I slept in Grandmama Rita's bed.

"I was looking through this book she made for me and didn't feel like walking all the way back to my bedroom, so I slept in here."

"I already made breakfast, Mama. BJ ate and is outside riding his bike with his friends."

"Okay. Thank you. I'm getting up now." When I got out of bed, Kyra sat and looked through the book. As I walked past the kitchen, I yelled back to her, "It smells good in here! What did you cook?"

"I made pancakes, eggs, and turkey links," she yelled back.

When I stepped out of the shower, Kyra was standing in my bedroom doorway. I thought, *"What is she up to now?"* I walked to my closet and said, "Kyra, I need my space so I can get dressed. I'm leaving early so I can stop by your dad's job. He needs my signature on some retirement papers."

"Is he going to retire?" she asked.

"No. Not yet. I need to sign some papers I should have signed a long time ago."

I walked out of the closet fully dressed, and Kyra stated, "Mama, you look very nice."

"Thank you," I replied with a smile and a twirl.

"Can you drop me off at Grandmama's house?"

"I thought you were going to stay home today with BJ."

"I told Grandmama I would help her today."

"Help her do what?"

"She has five dozen cookies to bake and two sheet cakes for a teacher who's retiring tonight."

"If you go, BJ has to go with you."

"Mama, he always follows behind me!" she said with exasperation.

"Kyra, he's your little brother. He loves being around you."
I headed to the kitchen to grab a bite to eat, with Kyra hot on my heels. We sat at the island, and I started eating my breakfast. "Kyra, this food is good! Thanks for cooking this morning."

"Mama, if I tell you something, will you get angry?"

"No. What is it?

"My friend Nathan said you're pretty and that I look just like you."

"Oh? He said that, huh? Well, tell him I said thank you. That's a compliment. Why would I get angry when someone is complimenting me?" I asked.

She nervously played with the salt shaker before speaking again. "When can I start dating?"

"Kyra, didn't your daddy tell you that you can start dating when you're sixteen?

"When I turn 16, will BJ still be following behind me?

"He probably will. What will you be doing that BJ can't be with you?"

"Mama, he gets on my nerves and talks too much."

"That's not nice to say."

"Zoe has a boyfriend, and I'm older than she is. Carlos doesn't follow her around. Their dad said if I were there, he would let me date, too."

I stopped eating and looked at her. "Everybody has rules in their house. In this house, the rule says you must be 16 in order to date."

"I should have asked daddy." I laughed at the expression she had on her face. "That's not funny, Mama."

"No, it's not funny, but you will not date until you are sixteen. Now, go get BJ so we can leave." I dropped them off and went to Bryce's office to sign the papers. When I arrived, I had to wait in the lounge because he was with a recruit. While waiting, I got a call from my friend Sherri, who lives in Baltimore, Maryland, asking me to speak at a women's convention in August, which happened to be the same weekend as Bryce's family reunion. I didn't commit to her request right then and there, but told her I would get back to her.

****

After ending the conversation with Sherri, I reflected on our friendship. We graduated from high school and enrolled in college together. I recalled the times she would visit me at my house and often give me rides to college when I was pregnant with Kyra. I remembered her encouraging me to tell my Mama I was pregnant, but I was afraid of her reaction. Funny thing: Brandon knew I was pregnant before he left home. One day, Sherri and I arrived at my house at the same time Mama was coming in from work at the hair salon. I could see the tiredness on her face as she walked in and headed straight to her bedroom. Sherri asked, "Are you going to tell her now?"

"No," I replied. "Have a seat. I'll go grab the book you left here." When I came back with the book, Mama was sitting in a chair across from Sherri, talking. I interrupted their conversation, saying, "Mama, I need to tell you something." I heard the tremble in my voice with each word I spoke.

She looked up at me and said, "Okay. What is it?" I was so nervous that the words wouldn't come out of my mouth, and my knees were shaking.

"She's trying to tell you that she's pregnant," Sherri chimed in, standing in the gap for me.

Mama squinted her eyes at me. "You're pregnant and in the church without a husband? Who is the baby's father?"

Sherri answered all the questions Mama asked. I could see the disappointment written all over her face. When Sherri left, Mama talked to me about having a baby out of wedlock and told me it wouldn't be easy raising a child alone. As she spoke, I sat there thinking, *"She doesn't know the whole story behind what happened to me, and I can't tell her."* I knew Mama wanted me to date a guy named Jay because his family went to our church, and his mother worked at the salon with her. After she found out I was pregnant, she reminded me almost every day that I had messed up my life and that she wasn't going to babysit my baby while I "ran the streets." The day Kyra was born, Mama and Sherri were with me in the hospital. Four months later, Sherri and Kelvin got married and moved to Baltimore. Two years later, Kelvin was appointed pastor of their church. Mama, Kyra, and I went to his ordination service.

****

My thoughts were interrupted when Bryce came in with the papers I needed to sign. He kissed me and said, "You are attracting attention today. The secretary told the other officers that there was a beautiful woman in here, waiting to see me, and they all had to peek and see who you were."

I laughed and replied, "I was wondering why all those men kept peeking at me."

He pulled me up from my seat and held me close. "You're beautiful, Babe." He kissed me again and asked, "Are the children home?"

"No, I dropped them off at your mom's house. She wanted Kyra to help her bake cakes and cookies. Bryce, Sherri called and asked me to come and speak in August, but it's around the same time as the reunion. I told her I'd get back to her. And you won't believe what your daughter asked me this morning." I told him about Kyra wanting to date.

While laughing, he said, "What? Looks like we need to have another talk with her about that."

"I can't believe she wants to date at fourteen. She's talking to Zoe way too much," I said, turning to walk out the door.

"Wait, Amber! You didn't sign the papers!" We burst out laughing. I signed on the dotted lines and then left.

Driving to work, I thought about the trial I was working on and then prayed. In court, everything went smoothly. Thankfully, it was a quick trial. We received the verdict, and I won the case. Bryce was already home when I pulled into the garage. When I walked into the house, I was greeted by a dozen roses sitting on the island in the kitchen. "What's the occasion? Why the roses?" I asked curiously.

"Babe, today is a special day! I'm home alone with my wife, I got three recruits, and I can't wait to get my check!" he answered with a broad smile.

I called Ms. Eva to let her know that we'd pick up the children around 7:00 because Bryce and I "had a little business to handle."

Bryce was shocked. "Wow, Babe! You told her that?"

"Yes, I did," I replied unashamedly.

"After you left my office today, I could hardly wait to get back home to you," he said as he retrieved two steak dinners from Outback from the oven. "Wash up so we can eat." After dinner, we had a little "playtime." Before going to pick up the children, Bryce suggested that we stop at KFC to grab dinner for Ms. Eva and them.

As we entered his mom's kitchen, she greeted us by saying, "I'm glad to see something other than cakes, cookies, and pies! We have been baking all day!" She then excused herself and left the kitchen.

"I want to open a bakery when I finish school. I enjoy baking," Kyra announced. "I am writing down every recipe and taking pictures of our baked goods, and then I plan to write a cookie cookbook."

"Are you still talking about that book and bakery?" Bryce asked.

"Yes, daddy. 'Eva's and Kyra's Bakery and Sandwich Shop'," she replied, laughing.

Bryce joined in the laughter and asked, "What happened to 'E & K Bakery'?"

"Eva and Kyra's Bakery sounds better," Kyra said pointedly.

Ms. Eva returned to the kitchen and asked, "What are you all talking about with my name in it?"

"Grandmama, we're talking about my future plans. You and I are going to open a bakery and sell sandwiches and soups," Kyra stated.

"Kyra, that sounds good. I'm praying that God blesses us with a bakery because we need a bigger space," she replied, laughing while fixing their dinner plates. "You know, Kyra is an excellent helper. I don't know what I would have done today if I didn't have her here to help me. She did a good job with those cookies, and she catches on fast. Tell BJ to come and wash his hands so we can eat."

On our ride home, Kyra's phone rang. I heard her say, "No, we are going to a family reunion after I come back from my cruise... Yes, I'm going on a cruise with my Grandmama and my girl cousins. When we get back, we're going to a family reunion in Alabama... For real? You are having a reunion in Alabama, too? Wow!"

"Kyra, who are you talking to?" I asked, annoyed by how openly she shared her plans.

"Zoe," she answered.

As soon as we pulled into the garage, Kyra hopped out of the car, still talking on the phone, and went into her bedroom. BJ went to his room to play his video game. I saw Bryce shaking his head as he walked into the house and sat in the family room. I went into my office to make a scheduled conference call.

A few minutes later, I heard Bryce yell, "Kyra, BJ, you guys take your showers and come down so we can pray." I finished the call and then joined Bryce on the couch. "I see Kyra talks a lot to her brother and sister," he said, his tone revealing how bothered he was by recent developments.

My tone matched his when I replied, "Yes. She talks to their dad, too, telling them everything that goes on here." Around that time, Kyra and BJ came into the family room. We talked to them about being obedient. BJ fell asleep, and Kyra was dozing off, so we ended our talk after about 15 minutes. We then prayed and went to bed. I quickly drifted off to sleep, only to be awakened by a knock on the bedroom door. "Who is it?" I asked. It was Kyra.

"It's me, mom. Are you going to work today?"

"No, Kyra. I don't have to go in today, and neither does your dad. Go back to bed."

By the time everyone got up, Kyra had breakfast ready. We spent the day cleaning the house, and then on Friday, we all worked on the outside, cleaning out the flowerbed, around the pool, and tidying the garage.

Early Saturday morning, Kyra knocked on our door, saying we didn't have to get up and that she would serve us breakfast in bed. "Not now," I replied. "Maybe around 10:30. Go back to your room for now. Don't wake your father." I had to stop and wonder, *"She's been extra nice lately. What is she up to?"* I then drifted off to sleep. At 9:00, there was another knock. "Who is it?" I called out.

"Mom, it's me again."

"Kyra, what do you want this time?"

She opened the door slowly and then climbed into the bed between Bryce and me. "I want to talk to both of you, and please don't say no."

"It's all based on what you have to say," I said.

"Well, my birthday is coming up, and..."

I cut her off. "That's four months away."

She continued. "I know, but I want to have my birthday party at a hotel this year." Neither Bryce nor I said a word. "Daddy, wake up. Mama, are y'all listening to me?"

"A birthday party in a hotel? No way, Jose!" Bryce said, finally breaking through the silence.

"But daddy, Zoe had a party at a hotel!"

"Who is supposed to come to this party?" I asked.

"Six people. Well, seven counting me. Carlos and Zoe said they wanted to come, too."

"So, you're telling me that Carlos and Zoe would come all the way from Michigan for a birthday party just for one day?" I asked, disbelief evident in my voice.

Before she could answer, Bryce held up his hand, getting Kyra's attention. "You can end this conversation right now, young lady. You are not having a party in a hotel room. If you have a party, it will be here."

"Zoe had her party at a hotel, and I'm older than her," Kyra pouted.

Bryce sat up and swung his legs over the side of the bed, clearly frustrated. "Girl, do you really think I'm going to let seven 14-year-olds go to a hotel room unsupervised? Like I said, no way, Jose."

"Daddy, you're just old-fashioned and stuck back in the '70s. I can't do anything I want to do. I have my own money and can pay for it myself."

"Kyra, you're not listening to me whatsoever, I see. I said you are not having a party in a hotel. Do you hear me?"

Without another word, she sprang out of bed and left the room, slamming the door behind her. "Get out of my way, little boy!" she yelled at BJ. The next thing I knew, she was in the kitchen, tossing pots and pans around and causing a big ruckus.

Bryce stormed out behind her. I heard him say, "I am not having that attitude in this house!"

Meanwhile, BJ came into my room and asked, "Mama, what's wrong with Kyra?"

"She's just having a meltdown over something she wants to do but can't. She'll be okay."

A few minutes later, Kyra came into my room and said, "Mama, I'm sorry." Then, she quickly turned around and walked out.

Bryce came back and told BJ to go into the family room and watch TV. "Oh, man!" he exclaimed as he left and closed the door behind him.

Bryce sat at the edge of the bed and rested his head in his hands. "Babe, she's got all this stuff in her head—talking about what Zoe and Carlos can do, along with whatever Carl has told her. I think she's spending way too much time on that phone with them. I told her to come and apologize to you and then go to her room. Did she apologize?"

"Yes, she did."

"It's going on 10:00. Get dressed. We're all going out for breakfast. I'm hungry."

"Is Kyra coming?"

"Yes. I believe she's had enough time to think about her behavior," he replied as he walked to the closet to get dressed.

I paused at Kyra's door to tell her we were all going out for breakfast. As I kept walking, I heard her talking on the phone, so I turned back. I heard her saying, "Girl, they're just tripping and so old-fashioned. I will be glad when I leave this house. I can't do anything. All I hear is no, no, no." I was standing in the doorway, listening to her side of the conversation. She must have felt someone behind her because she suddenly turned to see me there. My jaw nearly dropped when I saw her wearing red lipstick and false eyelashes, looking like she was 18, not fourteen.

"Kyra! Who are you talking to?" I asked. She just stood there, looking surprised. I took the phone from her hand, put it to my ear, and asked, "Who is this?"

"Zoe," came the reply.

"Well, Zoe, as of now, Kyra is on punishment for the next two weeks. There's no need for you to call. I will have her phone. Goodbye." I pressed the button to end the call and curled my hand tightly around Kyra's phone.

Kyra shouted, "Mama, you can't do that! All my numbers are in there!"

"Get in that bathroom and wash that mess off your face!" I shouted back.

"Zoe's daddy lets her wear makeup, and she's younger than me," she yelled.

"I'm not Zoe's daddy. Go wash that mess off your face now!" I yelled, matching her energy.

Just then, Bryce came in and asked, "What's taking you ladies so long? I'm ready to eat."

"Bryce, come in here and look at Kyra."

When he saw her, he stood there in disbelief. "Kyra, go wash your face, right now."

She began to cry as she stomped toward the bathroom and shouted, "I will be glad when I leave this house! I can't do anything here!"

"Where did you get that makeup from?" Bryce asked, already suspecting the answer.

"Zoe sent it to me," she replied through her tears.

"Throw it all in the trash! You know you're not old enough to be wearing makeup!"

I thrust her phone at her. "Here's your phone back. Call Zoe's daddy and tell him to send you a ticket. You can leave this house right now. I'm pregnant and refuse to let you stress me out. I'm getting tired of your mouth and attitude!"

"Amber, calm down. You don't mean that," Bryce said, pulling me close to him.

"Yes, I do! She's not going to have that man control what happens in this house. He has never done anything for her, and I don't like her attitude around BJ. If she doesn't want to be here, she can leave!" Kyra looked shocked at what I said. Bryce was surprised too.

"Kyra, are you coming to breakfast with us?" he asked.

"No. I don't want to go," she replied, still crying.

As soon as Bryce and I walked out, we heard her talking on the phone again. I stood in the family room for a moment, thought about her bad attitude, and returned to her room. "Did you just talk to Zoe's dad?"

"Yes, ma'am."

"Give me the phone back. Now."

"But Mama, I need my phone!" she whined. I took it from her hand and walked away.

I approached Bryce as he stood by the island in the kitchen. He looked at me thoughtfully before asking, "Do you think you should pray about the decision you made regarding Kyra leaving?"

"No, I don't. Let her go and live with strangers, and she'll see that the grass isn't greener on the other side. I'm nipping this thing before the bulb blooms."

"But Babe, what if she likes it there and doesn't want to come back home?" he asked with concern heavy in his voice.

"The Lord is my witness today: If that man sends her a ticket and she leaves, she'll be back before we know it. I know her spirit, Bryce. She needs to see what it's like for herself."

When we finally got in the car to head to breakfast, BJ asked, "What took you so long? And where is Kyra?"

I hesitated, waiting to see if Bryce would respond, but he didn't say a word. "She didn't want to come," I answered.

"She's always mean to me, calling me a little boy and saying I'm a blabbermouth."

"Sometimes, big sisters say mean things to their little brothers. She doesn't mean it," Bryce replied, looking at me.

"Mama, my friend Tae, who lives next door to Grandmama, wants me to come to his birthday party. Can I go?" BJ asked.

"See what your daddy says about that, BJ." Bryce didn't say a word. "Well, Bryce, can he go?"

He looked at me from the driver's seat and said, "That's your call. You're the one making decisions around here." I could tell he was upset with me by the way he responded.

At the restaurant, while we looked over the menu, BJ asked, "Daddy, do I have to pay for my breakfast?"

Bryce laughed and said, "No, I got it. Order whatever you want."

We placed our orders, and while waiting for the food to arrive, I excused myself and went to the bathroom. When I returned, Bryce was talking to someone on Kyra's phone. "Okay," he said into the receiver. "Here's Amber."

I put the phone to my ear, only to hear Kyra's father on the other end. He sounded angry when he said, "Zoe told me you put Kyra on punishment for talking to her..."

I cut him off. "I'm glad you called. I told Kyra she can come for a visit with you if you send her a ticket."

"I can send her a ticket today," he said angrily.

I was surprised that he said that! "Okay. Good. I'll let her know she will be leaving today." Bryce's eyes nearly popped out of their sockets when he heard what I had agreed to. Before hanging up, Carl said he would text the flight details to Kyra's phone. Bryce was furious. I didn't think for a second that Carl would agree to Kyra joining them, let alone buy the ticket. When I started to tell Bryce what was said, he cut me off by raising his hand and saying, "I heard you," as he shook his head in frustration.

After breakfast, Bryce called his Mama to ask about the party BJ was invited to. "We'll drop him off in a few minutes," I heard him say. When we arrived, he asked if I was coming in. I told him no, but to let Ms. Eva know I'd call her later. The two of them exited the car, and I closed my eyes and leaned back on the headrest, thinking about what I just did. Suddenly, I heard Ms. Eva call out, "Amber! Amber! You should have told Kyra to come over here. She's just going through some teenager stuff."

I opened my eyes and saw Bryce standing beside his mom, looking sad. "Ms. Eva, coming over here won't change her attitude. She needs to see for herself. Trust me," I replied. She didn't say anything else before turning around and walking slowly back into her house.

On our drive home, the only thing Bryce said to me was, "I wonder if he's planning on keeping my daughter."

As soon as we pulled into the garage, Kyra's phone beeped, indicating a text. I read it aloud: "This is information about Kyra's ticket. She leaves Dallas-Fort Worth today at 5:40 p.m."

"Today?" Bryce asked, alarmed.

"Yes, at 5:40 p.m., and she'll arrive in Detroit at 7:50 p.m. The text says he will be wearing a lime green shirt so that she'll recognize him." I sat there, looking at the phone and thinking, *"I didn't think he'd respond so quickly."* Meanwhile, I felt guilty about making Ms. Eva cry and upsetting Bryce.

Kyra was taking a pound cake out of the oven when we walked into the house. She knew her daddy loved her lemon pound cakes. She set the cake on the island and said, "I'm so sorry for the way I acted. Will y'all forgive me? Daddy, I'm not going to wear any more makeup until I'm 16, and I asked God to forgive me, too. Where is BJ?" she asked, looking around.

"He's at Grandmama's. Pack your clothes. You're flying out today at 5:40," I replied, the words rushing out of my mouth at lightning speed.

"Flying where?" she asked, surprised.

"You're going to your dad's house."

"Mama! Are you serious? You're sending me to visit with those people? I told you I was sorry!" Kyra's voice trembled with fear, even as I tried to stay emotionless.

"Hurry. You need to pack. The flight information is already on your phone. Just show it to the ticket agent. Don't forget to pack your phone charger," Bryce said, though I could hear the pain in his voice as well.

"I told y'all I was sorry!" she cried as Bryce turned and went into our bedroom and closed the door behind him.

"Let's go. Let me help you pack," I said. She slowly followed me into her room and took her luggage out of the closet. We packed her cute summer outfits and matching shoes.

"How long will I be there?" she asked.

"That's left up to you." Neither of us said a word as we packed enough clothes for a two-week stay. "Are you ready to go?" I asked.

She responded with the saddest tone I'd ever heard from her, "I think so, but let me grab a slice of daddy's cake. I'll eat it on the plane."

I called out to Bryce, telling him it was time to go. He stepped out with his shades on and said, "Give me a hug, princess. I hate to see you go." I could tell he had been crying. During our drive to the airport, he told her, "Don't forget to say your prayers every morning and night. And read a chapter in Proverbs every day."

"I will, daddy," she replied sadly.

After dropping her off at the airport and making sure she was safe, the drive home was dead silent, except for my sobs as I cried all the way. When we entered the house, Bryce went straight to Kyra's room, looking sad as he stood in the doorway. "She will be back sooner than you think," I whispered to him. He didn't reply. Instead, he went into the kitchen, got a slice of pound cake and a glass of milk, and then sat in the family room, enjoying his sweet treat in silence.

Recognizing he wanted to be alone, I went into our bedroom, cried some more, and read my Bible. Around 7:30, I took a shower and got into bed, reflecting on the events of the day. *"Did I really just send my daughter to stay with the man who forced himself on me, impregnated me, and abandoned her before she was born?"* I thought. I cried for a long time, thinking about those days. When Bryce walked in, I asked, "Are you picking up BJ tonight?"

"No. Mama said that after the party, he could spend the night with her," he replied as he headed to the bathroom, still looking very sad.

"Kyra's gone, and summer camp starts Monday. Who will be here to get BJ when he gets home every day?" I asked.

Coming out of the bathroom, he said, "I'll ask Mama tomorrow if he can get off the bus at her house. They don't have camp on Fridays." He sat on the bed and put his head in his hands. "Amber, you sent her away. She said she was sorry."

"She'll be a different child when she returns," I said confidently. He simply looked at me and shook his head before lying down on his side, turning away from me.

Around 8:30, the house phone rang. Bryce answered. It was Kyra, saying she had landed in Detroit but didn't see anyone with a lime green shirt. He put the call on speakerphone. "Go to baggage claim. He might be waiting for you there. We'll talk to you until you see him."

A few minutes later, we heard her ask, "Are you Carl?"

"Yes, I am. You must be Kyra. You are beautiful, just like I remember your mother looking."

"Bye, y'all! I'll call you tomorrow. I love you!" Kyra said hurriedly before hanging up.

When the phone went silent, I cried nonstop. Bryce tried to comfort me, but he was crying, too. I thought, *"Lord, did I do the right thing by sending her to Carl?"* That night, I cried myself to sleep.

The next morning, Bryce was already awake and making breakfast when I got up. I got dressed and went into the kitchen. He entered after stopping by the children's rooms. "Both of our children are gone. Is this how it's going to feel when they leave home?" he asked.

"No. We will still have a little one running around," I replied, rubbing my belly.

He kissed me on the cheek and said, 'Hurry up. We are going to be late for church."

At church, Bryce was asked to read from the Old Testament. He chose Psalm 1:1-6. The sermon was based on the Book of Jude, and the choir sang very well. The only thing missing was seeing Kyra up there singing. After the service, the pastor's wife came over to me and said, "I heard you sent my singing girl away."

"Mother Faraday, she will be back with a different attitude. This is just a test," I replied. She smiled and hugged me warmly.

On the way home, we went to Ms. Eva's house to pick up BJ. Walking in, she told us that Kyra had called and spoken with her and BJ, and that she'd call again tonight. Bryce asked her if BJ could get off the bus at her house tomorrow, as he is starting summer camp. "Yes, it's okay with me," she said.

"Amber or I will pick him up when we get off work." Monday afternoon, Bryce and I arrived at his Mama's house at the same time to pick up BJ.

"You should just let him stay here for the rest of the week," she suggested.

"No, Mama. You need some time to yourself without BJ," Bryce replied as he tried to hand her some money. She didn't want to take it, so he placed it on the table. We gave her hugs and then left.

Once home, BJ came into our room and said, "I miss Kyra. Why did she have to leave?" I talked with him and assured him that she would be back soon. Bryce told him to look in our closet for his new summer clothes. He had six new outfits and a pair of Jordan tennis shoes. BJ was thrilled!

He hugged both of us and asked, "Did y'all get Kyra new clothes, too?"

"Yes, we did. She took them with her," I answered.

"Can I wear one of my new outfits tomorrow?"

"Yes, you can," Bryce replied. BJ was so happy as he left our room.

Just as Bryce and I were falling asleep, Kyra called. I answered and put her on speaker. She asked, "Where's daddy?"

"He's right here. He can hear you."

"Daddy, why did you let Mama send me here?" We could tell she was crying.

"Kyra, I didn't have anything to do with it. That was between you and your mama," he replied.

"I told y'all I was sorry, but you still sent me here!" She was nearly hysterical.

I spoke up and said, "That's where I thought you wanted to be."

"Mama, I told you I was sorry. I'm ready to come home."

"But you just got there!"

"I don't know these people. Daddy, why aren't you saying anything?" From her end, we heard a woman's voice calling her name. "I gotta go. That lady is calling me," she said, quickly hanging up the phone.

Bryce was so hurt, hearing her cry. "Lord, please protect my daughter," he prayed.

The next day, while waiting for my lunch to be delivered at work, I got a call from Bryce. "Amber, I don't like hearing Kyra crying to come home. I can send her a return trip ticket," he said sadly.

"Bryce, she will be okay. She's not broken yet. We'll talk about this when I get home. My lunch is here, and I need to review this case before going back to court. I love you. See you soon," I replied, hanging up.

That evening, Bryce picked up dinner on his way home. During our meal, he didn't say anything about Kyra. BJ did most of the talking, telling us about a field trip at the end of summer camp to the Dallas World Aquarium. "Now, I can't go because

Kyra isn't here to go with me," he said with disappointment. Bryce told him he would sign the permission slip and go with him instead. "Mama, can you come with us, too?"

That's a lot of walking, BJ. I'll see how I'm feeling, okay?" He nodded and refocused on his pizza. After dinner, I cleaned the kitchen while Bryce and BJ went outside to power wash the house. Then I went to lie down in the bedroom to rest. I heard them come in and settle in the family room to watch a movie. Later, Bryce came into the room and asked if I was asleep. "No, I'm awake. Just lying here, thinking about how big my belly is."

He came over, rubbed my belly, and said, "My little boy is growing big."

"How do you know this baby is a boy?"

He laughed and responded, "I just know," as he walked toward the bathroom.

"We will find out at my next doctor's visit!" I shouted after him

Wednesday morning, I didn't feel well when I woke up. I prayed and went to work anyway. Around 10:00, I started feeling weak and dizzy, but I was assigned to sit in on a mediation hearing. After the hearing, I went home, got into bed, and fell asleep. My sleep was interrupted when Bryce called to tell me he was at his Mama's house fixing a light in her bathroom. A few minutes later, the house phone rang again. I didn't recognize the number, so I let it go to voicemail. I heard a voice say, "Mama, daddy, pick up the phone. It's me. Kyra." When I picked up, she said, "Mama, Carl wants to talk to you." She sounded excited.

"Hi, Amber," Carl began. "I'm calling to thank you for letting Kyra come for a visit. When I first saw her at the airport, it was as if I were looking at you. She's beautiful. When we got home, I showed her the picture we took together."

"What picture?" I asked.

He laughed as he replied, "The picture we took when our class went to Six Flags."

"You were Mr. Football and took pictures with a lot of girls. Why did you keep that one with me in it? You didn't even know me."

As if trying to impress Kyra, he said, "There are two other girls in it with us."

"Were the other two girls a notch on your belt like I was?" I asked, not hiding my disdain for him. His laughter stopped immediately, and his end of the line went silent. I didn't know if he had me on speakerphone or not, but I continued the conversation. "Why are you silent? Are you remembering what you did to me?" The silence was deafening.

Finally, he cleared his throat and said, "Kyra is ready to come home. I have a meeting in Detroit tomorrow, so I'll put her on the plane at 9:40 a.m. our time. She should arrive there at 11:42 your time."

"Okay. Let Kyra know that either her father or I will be there to pick her up. Bye." After ending the call, I remained in bed, thinking, *"Lord, how am I supposed to feel toward the man who forced himself on me, trying to win a bet?"* Then, I thought about Kyra and prayed aloud, "Lord, I thank you for giving her to me. Thank you for sending her back home. I pray she has learned her lesson. Lord, bless her with a safe trip. Amen."

I was still in bed when Bryce got home. "Babe? Where are you?" he called out.

"I'm in the bedroom."

He entered the room and asked, "Why are you in bed so early? Are you waiting for me?" He laughed as he planted a kiss on my lips.

"No, I came home early from work because I don't feel well."

"Why didn't you call me? Did you eat anything yet?"

"No, I wasn't hungry."

"Well, Mama sent you some vegetable soup and cornbread. It's good. Maybe you need to eat something, and then you'll feel better."

"Please bring me a bowl and a small piece of cornbread. When you get back, I have something to tell you." As he walked out, I yelled, "Where is BJ?"

"Mama wanted him to stay with her since Kyra isn't here. Is that okay with you?"

"Yes, that's fine. Please hurry with my food!"

"I'm coming!" he said, entering the room with the tray of food. "I added a bowl of fresh fruit."

"Thank you, Hon. Now, what I'm about to tell you, you're going to shout for joy."

"What is it?" He was anxiously waiting for me to tell him, but I started eating my food instead.

"This soup is delicious. I must call your mom and thank her for the food," I teased, knowing he was waiting to hear my good news.

"Amber, stop taunting me! What do you have to tell me?"

I patted a spot on the bed beside me. "You're going to want to have a seat for this one." As soon as he got settled, I said, "Kyra is coming home tomorrow."

"For real?" he asked, a moment of uncertainty flashing across his face."

"Yes, for real. Tomorrow morning."

He fell back on the bed and said, "Thank you, Jesus!" He turned to me and asked, "What time will she arrive?"

"If the plane lands on time, 11:42."

Bryce was smiling from ear to ear. "Okay. I'll pick her up, but she'll have to go back to work with me because I have an appointment at 1:00." He stood and did a happy dance. "Lord, I thank you! Our baby girl is coming home!" I fell back asleep and woke up around 9:30 to Bryce watching the news. "How are you feeling now?" he asked.

"Much better since eating."

"You were hungry, Babe! You better feed my baby boy," he said, laughing. He pulled me close and rubbed my belly. "You know, I was so excited to hear your news that I forgot to tell you mine. The police officer working Sarah's case stopped by today and said Sarah is incompetent to stand trial. They are moving her to a mental health facility somewhere north of here. Maybe she'll finally get the help she needs and leave us alone."

When I woke up the next morning, Bryce had already left for work. I went to the kitchen and read the note he left for me that read: "Eat. I don't want you to be sick when Kyra gets home. I will call you after I pick her up. I love you." I sat at the island and ate the breakfast he made for me: a bowl of oatmeal, a boiled egg, toast, and a glass of orange juice. I then got dressed and went to work.

During my lunch break, Bryce called. "I got her," he reported. I could hear the happiness in his voice.

"Hi, Mama!" Kyra said happily. "I'm so excited to be home. I can't wait to see you!"

"I can't wait to see you either," I said sincerely. On my way home, I stopped by a Chinese restaurant and picked up dinner.

As they pulled into the garage, I opened the door. Kyra was the first one out of the car. She ran to me, hugged me, and said, "I am so glad to see you and happy to be home. I'm never leaving here again!" She went inside and examined every room in the house. When she came back, she said, "Everything is still the same!" We all laughed at her.

"Kyra, you were only gone for five days and four nights," Bryce reminded her.

"It seemed like a lifetime, daddy!" She even hugged BJ and told him she missed him.

"I missed you, too," he replied.

Bryce and I stood there, watching our children hug each other. "I smell food. I'm ready to eat," Bryce said.

"Everybody, wash your hands. The food is ready," I stated, rubbing my belly. "We're hungry!" We all laughed.

We all sat at the island, eating and listening to Kyra share stories about her trip. After dinner, she called Carl to let him know she had made it home. I heard her say, "Thanks for everything," before hanging up.

We then gathered in the family room for Bible study. We read through the Book of Colossians, and the children had to memorize one verse. Afterward, we played games. It was as if Kyra had never gone away.

I went into my bedroom, thanking God for bringing Kyra back home safe. Then I called Sherri to let her know I was pregnant and wouldn't be able to attend the convention.

"So, you are pregnant?" she asked.

"Yes, soon to be seven months."

"I'm pregnant, too!"

"For real, Sherri?"

"Yes. I actually postponed the convention and told Kelvin that when I finished grading these papers tonight, I was going to call and let you know."

"So, we're both having a baby this year? Wait. How many months are you?" I asked excitedly.

"I'm eight months along."

"Congratulations, Sherri! Listen, I'll let you go so you can finish up. We'll talk later. Take care of yourself."

"You, too," she said, ending the call.

Just then, Kyra walked into my bedroom. "Are you going to day camp with BJ tomorrow?" I asked.

Bryce walked out of the closet after putting on his nightclothes, saying, "Kyra, tell your Mama about your new job."

"You got a job? Doing what?"

"Organizing offices," Kyra said proudly.

"Really? Whose office are you organizing?" I asked, chuckling.

"I did daddy's office today. Then, two other recruiters saw what I had done and asked me to do theirs!"

"Babe, she did a really good job. She asked me if she could do the other two offices tomorrow, but I told her only if it was okay with you."

I had a big smile on my face when I replied, "It's okay with me, as long as your father is there and the doors to the offices stay open." Kyra jumped up and down with joy.

"Okay, Kyra. It's official! Be ready to leave at 7:30, and please dress appropriately," Bryce reminded her.

"I will. Goodnight!" she said, closing the door behind her.

I woke up early the next morning and made breakfast. I ate, then waited to see Kyra off to her first day at work. She was so happy to go in with her daddy. BJ went, too, since he didn't have summer camp on Fridays. After they left, I got dressed for work. As I was getting ready to leave, I opened the garage door and noticed a black Chrysler 300 sitting in front of our house. I could see someone inside. "Why is there a car sitting in front of our house?" I wondered.

A man got out and walked up the driveway. He was a Black man, about six feet tall, dressed in blue jeans and a pullover sweater, with dreadlocks and a beard, wearing a baseball cap and sunglasses. I got out of my car, standing with the door open. "Are you looking for someone?" I asked.

He hesitated and then replied, "Yes, I am."

The man's voice sounded familiar, but I couldn't remember where I'd heard it. "Who are you looking for?"

"You," he answered. I turned to get back in my car. He laughed and said, "Amber Rose, the last time I saw you, you were pregnant, but not that big."

"Oh, my God! Brandon? Is that you? It's been a long time, big brother! Almost 15 years!"

He hugged me and said, "Yes, it's me." I cried a flood of tears. I was so glad to see him. "Amber, you are looking good. Is Mama in the house?"

"No, she lives in Hampton, Virginia. She left here to be with Aunt Edna 12 years ago after Uncle Otis died and ended up staying with her. I'm sorry to say Aunt Edna died about six months ago. Mama was here for three weeks but went back to Virginia."

"I went by our old house. A man answered the door and told me he owned that house and that the lady he bought it from lived with her daughter on Red Bird Circle Drive, but he didn't know the exact address," Brandon said.

I glanced at my watch. "I'm sorry, Brandon. I have to be in the courtroom in an hour. Can you come back around 6:00 for dinner to meet my husband and children?"

"You work in the courts?"

"Yes, big brother. I'm a lawyer."

He laughed. "I'm proud of you, sis." He hugged me and said, "I will see you all at 6:00!"

Immediately after my trial, I called Bryce to check on how Kyra was doing at work. "She's doing great! She finished the first recruiter's office and told him, 'If you put things back where you get them, your office wouldn't be so junky.'" Both of us burst out laughing. "She also made a sign and taped it over his filing cabinet that reads: 'If you opened it, close it back. If you take it out, put it back where you got it from. If you drop it, pick it up.'" By then, we were both laughing hysterically.

"No, she didn't tell that man that!" I replied, still cracking up.

"Babe, not only did she tell me that, but she also put one of those signs on my filing cabinet this morning! She wrote it on red construction paper. Can't miss it!" When our laughter died down, I told him my brother was coming over for dinner. "That's great! I can't wait to meet him," he replied. "Babe, I gotta run and check on Kyra. I love you. Bye!"

I worked in the office until 1:00 p.m. that day and then went home to start dinner. I made a pot roast with all the fixings, and a lemon pie for dessert. I remembered how much Brandon loved lemon-flavored desserts.

A few minutes after 5:00, Bryce and the children arrived home. Kyra was the first to come inside, laughing hysterically. "Mama, we went by Grandmama's house. BJ stayed outside, playing with the dog, while daddy went inside to change the lightbulb in her ceiling fan. When we were getting ready to leave, we got into the car, and daddy asked, 'What's that smell?' It turned out that BJ had dog poop all over the back of his shirt and shorts. Daddy yelled, 'Boy, get out of my car!' Mama, it was all over the car seat. Grandmama came out to help him clean it and told BJ to go change his clothes!"

"I'm glad I have leather seats because that smell was horrible!" Bryce added, laughing. "What's for dinner, Babe? It smells good up in here!" He lifted the lid on the pot roast to have a peek.

"Wash your hands!" I yelled. "Kyra, how was your day at work?

"It was good, but I know one thing: men don't put stuff back where they get it from." Bryce was laughing so hard at what she said. "Mama, if daddy pays me, I'll make $80.00 this week. I'm saving my money for the cruise."

"Yes, that time is coming up quickly," Bryce replied.

"In half an hour, we're going to have a houseguest. You guys better be on your best behavior," I warned.

Right at 6:00, Brandon rang the doorbell. "I know you thought I wasn't coming back," he said jokingly.

"No, I never thought that. Come in and meet my family." Before sitting down to eat dinner, we gathered in the family room and talked. I liked how Bryce and Brandon got along. I excused myself to set the table and then told everyone to wash their hands and come to the table for dinner. Bryce blessed the food.

Brandon sniffed the air and asked, "Amber, did you make a lemon pie?"

"Yes, I did. I remembered how much you liked my lemon pies."

He chuckled and replied, "I think that was the only thing you knew how to make!" We all enjoyed a good laugh at that one. While eating dinner, Brandon told us he was on a secret job assignment and that since he was in the States, he decided to visit Mama and me. "Amber, could you call Mama for me?" he asked after dinner.

"Yes. Follow me back to her room." He complimented me on the rooms in the house and took a seat on a stool at the bar, looking through the book Mama made me. "This is Mama's living quarters whenever she comes to visit."

He smiled and said, "This isn't a long visit, Amber. You and two other people know I'm in town. I'm working on a high-profile case out of Houston. We got a lead that led us here. That's what I've been doing all day, following that lead."

I put my hand up to stop him from speaking. "Okay, Brandon. You don't have to tell me anything else." We sat and reminisced about the things we did when we were growing up. "I heard you tell BJ about your children. Are you married?"

"Yes, I am. My wife's name is Sue Lee," he said, showing me a picture of his family. "Hopefully, in five years, all of this chasing will be behind me. I'm trying to get my orders changed so I can come back to the States. Please call Mama now."

I called her and put her on the TV monitor. "Is everything alright?" she asked. "You normally call me on the weekend."

"Everything's okay, Mama. Guess who stopped by our house this morning and came back for dinner? He wants to see you," I teased.

"I don't know, but let me comb my hair before anybody sees me!" she said, laughing. I watched as she combed her hair while we talked. "Okay. Now, I'm ready." I turned the monitor toward Brandon. "Who is that?" she asked.

"Mama, it's me! Brandon!" he said, cracking up.

"You don't look like Brandon."

"Mama, when you got the news about daddy, I was seven. Do you remember what happened to me?"

"Yes, I remember what happened to Brandon," she replied, still not convinced this man was her son.

Brandon kept talking. "I ran out of the house, climbed that big tree in front of our house, and then fell. You had to take me to the hospital. Look, Mama. I still have the scar," he said, pulling up his sweater to show her the scar on his side.

"Brandon! It is you!" Then, she began to cry. I left the room to give her some time alone with her son. A little while later, I came back to the room. He was off the phone and looking through the book again. "Mama said she will talk to you this weekend. She told me she made me a book like yours, but it doesn't have a cassette or locket with it. Could you make me a copy of both? I'll contact you when I can to let you know where to send them."

Our conversation was briefly interrupted when Brandon received a call. He answered and spoke a few words in Spanish before hanging up. "Well, my job is done. They'll meet me at the airport at midnight. That's all I can tell you."

I laughed and said, "I understood everything you said. Remember, I speak Spanish and French."

"That call will be our little secret, okay?" he whispered.

"Yes, our little secret."

Brandon and I rejoined the rest of the family and gathered for prayer, asking God to protect Brandon on his travels. He left shortly afterward. I felt sad to see him go, but I was glad he thought enough of me to stop by for a visit. I went to our bedroom while Bryce spent some more time with the children, painting a paint-by-number picture for Ms. Eva.

When Bryce got into bed, he said, "I enjoyed meeting your brother. He's a cool guy."

"Yes, he is. I was happy he got to talk to Mama. She's been worried about him."

"The children are in their room now. We're almost done with the painting. We only have three more numbers to paint, and then we'll be finished. You know, it looks really good. I'm going to ask Officer Don where he got it and buy three more; one for Allen, Rachel, and your mom. I'm pretty sure we can have hers finished before she visits again."

"Bryce, that's a good idea! I can frame it and have it hung in her room."

"Are you sleepy yet?" he asked as he sang "Baby, I Need Your Loving" in my ear. I nodded yes, and we settled in for the night.

On Friday, the children went to work with Bryce. I had to be in court at 9:00. By the time I arrived home that afternoon, my family was already there. Kyra made a taco salad for dinner while Bryce and BJ finished the painting. I must admit, they did a great job! I grabbed a bowl of salad and headed to my bedroom, feeling exhausted. Shortly after I finished eating, all of them ended up in our bed, with the children telling us about their day.

Early Saturday morning, we left the house so the cleaning crew could come and handle the monthly cleaning. We went out for breakfast and then ended up at the mall. I sat in the mall way, watching Bryce patiently interact with the children. A sudden thought flashed through my mind: "Kyra hasn't had much to say about Zoe since returning home. Did she tell Bryce that Zoe was acting jealous of her?" I was grateful to God that sending her away worked to correct her attitude. Leaving the mall, our final stop before heading home was the market, where everybody got what they wanted to eat for dinner. Once home, I ate and went straight to bed. Bryce came in, concern evident on his face, asking if I was okay and wondering why I was in bed so early. "My body is letting me know I'm too old to be having a baby. You did this to me!" I joked.

He laughed for a long time before replying, "You're not old! You're only thirty-three!"

"I know, but I feel much older than that right now."

Kyra came into our room, holding up two dresses, and asked which one she should wear to church tomorrow. Bryce chose one, and she seemed happy with his decision. She said goodnight and closed the door. "I can see a difference in her since she got back. Her attitude has changed quite a bit," he observed.

"I noticed that, too. I guess after being away from home with strangers, she realizes things aren't how she thought they'd be. Did she tell you Zoe was acting jealous of her?" I asked.

"No, but she told me Zoe tried to embarrass her in front of her friends by pulling her hair and laughing about it. I asked her how she felt about Zoe doing that, and she said, 'It hurt when she pulled my hair, but I know I look better than her. My hair is longer than hers. I know because she wears hair extensions. She's a Humpty-Dumpty. I was just ready to come home after that.' I explained to her that she was taking attention away from Zoe, making her feel left out." We spent a few more minutes comparing notes about what Kyra did and did not tell Bryce and me.

On Sunday morning, we went to church. The youth department was assigned to oversee the service. To our surprise, BJ was on the program to read the Old Testament scripture, and Kyra, along with two other girls, performed a praise dance. After church, we all went to Golden Corral, including Ms. Eva. While eating, I complimented BJ on his scripture reading and asked Kyra where she had gotten the beautiful praise dance outfit.

"Grandmama and I made it!" she said proudly.

"Ms. Eva, how much do we owe you for making that for Kyra?"

"You don't owe me a thing. Kyra and I are in business together. We'll just leave it at that," she replied, winking at Kyra.

After dinner, we dropped Ms. Eva off at her house. Before getting out of the car, Bryce invited her to our place for the 4th of July. The children asked her to make her punch bowl cake and seven-layer salad. Ms. Eva asked if it was okay to bring a friend. "Mama, you can bring anybody you'd like," Bryce replied.

On the way home, BJ announced, "Grandmama has a boyfriend."

"That's not her boyfriend, BJ. It's just Brother Goodman from the church. She talks to him all the time," Kyra replied.

Bryce didn't say anything, but the puzzled look on his face spoke volumes. As we pulled into the garage, he asked, "Kyra, did you finish organizing all the offices at work?"

"Yes, I did, and they told me before I go back to school, I can come and do them again."

"So, Babe, what do you think about our daughter having a part-time job?" he said, laughing.

"As long as you're there, it's okay with me!" That reply had Kyra happily bouncing into the house.

On Monday morning, I woke up to the smell of food cooking. Although Kyra didn't have to get up early, she was busy working in the kitchen. When I walked in, I asked, "Why are you up so early?" Bryce had already finished his breakfast and was getting ready to leave for work.

"I was hungry, Mama. Once I eat, I'm going back to bed."

"Thanks for breakfast, princess. It was good," Bryce said. He gave me a kiss and kissed Kyra on her forehead before heading out the door.

Kyra yelled behind him, "When you get home, I want to talk to you!"

"Oh, my goodness. Here we go again!" he replied, laughing as he closed the door.

A little later, it was time for me to head to work. "I'll see you two in a little while. Remember, daddy has cameras watching you." On my way to work, I prayed for my family and thanked God for Bryce. He was such a good husband and father. I thought about the look on his face when BJ said Ms. Eva had a boyfriend. He was so protective of her that I don't know how he would react if she did, indeed, have a boyfriend.

On the 4th, Bryce was up early, grilling the meats. I made baked beans and potato salad as sides. At 3:00, Ms. Eva arrived with Bro. Goodman and another woman. When Bryce saw the woman, he said, "Ms. Abby Alexander, how are you? I haven't seen you since before I went into the Navy." He shook Bro. Goodman's hand and welcomed everyone inside. Ms. Eva didn't come empty-handed; she brought the cake and salad the children requested, and Bro. Goodman added a watermelon to the spread.

At 3:30, Bryce's friend Terry arrived with his wife D'Ericka and their three children: twin eight-year-olds, Cass and Carson, along with a girl the same age as Kyra named Aniyah. D'Ericka carried coleslaw and a fruit salad, which I took and placed in the kitchen. The children played in the pool while the adults watched over them and chatted. Everyone stayed to enjoy the neighborhood fireworks display. When it was time to leave, I made sure everyone took some food home with them.

In bed that night, Bryce said, "It was good to see Ms. Abby. Her son Titus and I were best friends when we were in school. I wonder if Mama has anything going on with Deacon Goodman."

"I think he's just a friend, someone for her to talk to. Do you remember when, before we got married, I came over to pick you up for breakfast, and then afterward, we were going to pick up your car? Your mom asked where we were going. When you told her, she said, 'I don't want you fornicating around here. God sees everything.' I was so embarrassed, Bryce. She thought we were having sex, but we were just friends!"

He was laughing so hard. "Yes, Mama sure did say that!" There was a sudden knock on the door. "Who is it?"

"It's me, daddy."

"Come in, Kyra." She climbed into the bed between us, just like she had since she was four years old. "So, what do you want to talk to us about? It's after 11:00."

She sighed before speaking. "I know I acted up the last time we talked about my birthday, but I'm not that person anymore. I want to invite my new friend, Aniyah, a few friends from school, and a couple of boys from my Saturday Bible class to a party here at home. It'll be a simple party, just some fun food and a birthday cake. For my gift from you two, I want a fancy dinner, and daddy, you can take us all to Cedar Point in Ohio." She paused, waiting for Bryce to respond.

"Okay. Goodnight, Kyra," he murmured. "Tell us more about your plans tomorrow." She kissed us both on the cheek before leaving the room.

On Friday afternoon, as I left for work and got into my SUV, I realized I had left my phone plugged in at my office. I ran back inside to get it and received a FaceTime call from Bryce, who let me know he was at his Mama's house, fixing a leak under the sink. I told him I was leaving work and would pick up dinner on my way home.

Suddenly, someone covered my mouth. I woke up in a room with black curtains, and my hands and feet were tied. The room was dimly lit, and I saw a white dress hanging on a closet door. I yelled, "Help me! Somebody, help me!"

The door opened, and a strange man entered. He was Black, had a full beard, and weighed about 180 pounds. He wore dark blue clothes, a cap, and dark glasses. He placed a gag in my mouth and said, "Nobody can hear you. I got you now. I have the crib waiting for our baby." I started to cry and pray. I had no idea where I was, but I knew I had a tracker on my phone, hoping that Bryce would be able to find me. The man stood in front of me, laughing and rubbing my belly. "When I come back, I want you to put on that dress," he said, pointing to the dress. "We're going to get married." He walked out, locking the door behind him.

I prayed, "Lord, please don't let him hurt me or take my baby." I was terrified and needed to use the bathroom. To get the man's attention, I started kicking the chair and knocking it against the wall. I could hear a TV playing in the distance in another room. A few minutes later, the door opened slowly. I nodded my head toward the bathroom. He untied my hands, helped me into the bathroom, and closed the door behind me. I wanted to remove the gag from my mouth and scream, but it wouldn't have mattered. No one would hear me, and there was no window. I heard him moving something around in the room, thinking he was blocking my exit from the bathroom. When I was done, I knocked on the door. He opened it, led me back to the chair, and retied my hands. The noise was him dragging a dresser to block the room's only window.

He walked out, locking the door behind him once again. A little while later, the doorbell rang repeatedly. I thought, *'Thank you, Lord! Someone is here!"* Unfortunately, help did not arrive. A few minutes later, the man entered the room with a box of KFC. "I hope you like fried chicken, mashed potatoes, and coleslaw," he said, looking at me with a big smile. "Let me get you something to drink." He left and locked the door... again.

I sat there, looking at the food, but my mouth was still gagged, and my hands and feet were still tied. I heard the doorbell ring again, followed by a loud boom. "Amber! Where are you?" It was Bryce! He found me! Thank you, Lord! I couldn't answer him because of the gag in my mouth. I heard voices approaching and saw the doorknob turning. When it wouldn't open, it was kicked in. I was so happy to see my husband. He removed the gag from my mouth and held me close as I cried uncontrollably. "Are you alright? Did he hurt you?" he asked as he hurriedly untied my hands and feet.

"No," I replied through tears.

"Thank God we have trackers on our phones. I called right back, but it went to voicemail."

"What took you so long to get here?" I asked.

"I stopped by your job first to check if you were still there. That's when I saw your SUV and found your purse on the seat. I called the police and told them you had been kidnapped."

"Did you see my phone?"

"No. That man must have it on him or in his van. That's how we tracked you here."

As we were leaving the house, I heard Kyra's ringtone coming from the man's van. I shouted, "That's my phone ringing!" One of the police officers opened the van door and found my phone on the floor.

Bryce turned to the man and said, "Man, you are sick." His hand was balled up into a fist, prepared to strike the man, but the police stood between them. The man just stood there in handcuffs, smiling.

I answered Kyra's call. "Mama, where are you? And where is daddy? Grandmama is waiting for him."

"We're on our way," I replied through tears as I ended the call. My knees were shaking so badly I could barely walk. The officer asked if I wanted to go to the hospital. "No. I'm okay."

As Bryce guided me to his car, he repeatedly said, "You're safe. Thank you, Jesus." He took me to get my SUV from work, asked me to drive straight home, and said he would pick up dinner and meet me at the house. I entered the garage and waited for Bryce to arrive. While sitting there, I thought about that man. I remembered seeing him a few weeks earlier. He was in the elevator with a coworker of mine and me. On Wednesday, he spoke to me as he was getting out of his van. I thought, *"Oh, my God! He's been watching me all this time! Lord, I thank you for Bryce putting trackers on our phones."* When Bryce pulled up behind me, I was still too nervous to get out of my SUV. He had to help me walk to his car. I started crying again, saying, "Bryce, he rubbed my belly."

"He put his hands on you?" he yelled.

"Yes, and he said he had a crib ready for our baby. I saw the crib as we were leaving."

"Amber, you are safe now. The Lord blessed us to find you. Please stop crying. You are going to make yourself sick," he replied, trying to calm me down.

Thankfully, by the time we arrived at his mom's house with the food, my tears had dried up, and the children didn't notice I had been crying. They were busy telling us about a mouse BJ had caught on the patio that had their Grandmama running. We had a good laugh about it while eating our food. When I finished eating, I suddenly felt nauseous. I ran to the bathroom and vomited. Bryce came in behind me and asked, "Are you alright?"

"My stomach is upset."

Ms. Eva came in to see what was wrong with me. All the while, the children thought the food had made me sick. It was then that Bryce told his mom what happened. She hugged me tightly and said, "Come and lie down." I laid back on the couch while Bryce went into the kitchen to finish working on the sink. Ms. Eva sat on the couch with me, rubbing my hair. "Lord, I thank You for bringing Amber home safe," she prayed.

On our ride home, Bryce instructed the children always to be aware of their surroundings and specifically told Kyra to keep her phone charged and with her. He didn't tell them what happened to me earlier that day.

Pulling into the garage, I said, "I thank God the weekend is here. I don't want anybody to wake me up. I just want to sleep." They all laughed as we entered the house.

The first thing Monday morning, I went to the police station and pressed charges against that man. I left there and went to work. I felt nervous and didn't want to be there. The trial was scheduled to start at 10. It was a short trial. Immediately after the judge gave his verdict, I went to my office to get my purse and then drove myself to the hospital. I called Bryce to let him know I was there. After seeing the doctor, I called him again and asked him to come get me because I was too nervous to drive. He had an Uber drop him off, and he drove me home. During our drive, it started raining hard, so Bryce pulled over under an overpass, waiting for the rain to slow down. He sat there, looking at me. "Why are you looking at me like that?" I asked.

He started laughing. "Do you remember the first day I saw you when I got home from the Navy? You and Kyra came over for dinner. When you got out of your car, I watched you walk up and thought to myself, 'She is so beautiful.' Looking at you now, you are more beautiful than you were when I first saw you."

"Thanks for saying that, because I don't feel beautiful. I feel like crap."

We stayed under the overpass for about 30 minutes until the rain eased enough for us to drive home. When we arrived, Kyra and BJ were waiting at the door. Ms. Eva had dropped off a pot of homemade chicken noodle soup. During the week I was at home recovering, someone was there to take care of me every day. While Ms. Eva was there, she cooked, cleaned, and insisted I rest. That Friday, Bryce and BJ went on the camp field trip to the aquarium, and Kyra stayed home with me.

My mind flashed back to the kidnapping. I got so nervous, tears ran down my face. When Kyra walked into my room, she asked, "Mama, what's wrong?"

"I just need a hug," I replied.

She walked over and asked, "Do you want me to call daddy?"

"No, I need a hug from you." She smiled and gave me a long hug.

On Monday, I called my office and handed all my cases to a lawyer I had worked with before. I told her I wouldn't be back until after my baby was born. During my check-up with the doctor, I was told that both the baby and I were doing well, but I needed to rest and stay off my feet. The next week, Kyra and Ms. Eva started getting ready for their cruise, and Bryce prepared for his job in Alabama. He told me to pack and said that BJ and I could stay with him once we arrived in Alabama. All three paintings were finished, and Bryce mentioned we'd have them framed while we were there.

That Saturday, we left for Montgomery, Alabama, at 5:00 a.m. We picked up Ms. Eva, prayed for a safe trip, and hit the road. I enjoyed listening to Bryce and his Mama talk. Around 9:30, we stopped at McDonald's for breakfast and gas. Once back on the road, we heard BJ ask Kyra, "When Mama kissed daddy, is that how the baby got in her stomach?"

"BJ, who told you that?" Kyra asked.

"Raymond." Then he told her what Raymond told him about how babies are made.

"You need to stop listening to him. That's not true."

Around 2:30, we stopped for gas and a bathroom break. We were grateful for the food Ms. Eva brought along, saving us some money along the way. "Amber, I made some vegetable soup that you can heat up in your hotel room."

"Thank you," I said as I hugged her.

"Mama, I'm glad you brought this food! It hit the spot," Bryce said.

When we got back on the road, I drove while Bryce took a nap. I heard BJ talking, asking Kyra how they would get the baby out of my stomach. I looked in the rearview mirror and saw Ms. Eva laughing at their conversation. I drove until we were about 40 miles outside the Alabama state line. Bryce woke up when I pulled off for a bathroom break, and he drove the rest of the way to Allen's house.

After greeting everyone and dropping off Ms. Eva and Kyra, we left, telling them we'd be back tomorrow before they were scheduled to board the ship. We then drove to the Airbnb where we were staying: a nice two-bedroom, two-bath house with a living room, dining area, and kitchen. Bryce and BJ went to find a store to get breakfast and snack foods. I ate my vegetable soup, took a hot shower, and relaxed in bed until they returned.

On Sunday morning, we all slept in late and got up around 11:00. We had devotion, got dressed, and went to Cracker Barrel for a late breakfast. Afterward, we looked for the recruiting office where Bryce would be working, then went sightseeing. Later, we headed to Allen's house to see Ms. Eva and Kyra before they left on their cruise. When we arrived, Ms. Eva and the girls were excited and ready to go. Kyra rode with us to the ship. When we reached the boarding deck, she hugged us and said she loved us. She then turned to BJ and told him she was going to miss him while giving him a hug. As she walked away, Bryce called out, "Don't forget to pray!"

"I know, dad!" she yelled back. We stayed there until they were all safe on the ship.

As we drove back to the Airbnb, BJ started crying and said, "I never get to go anywhere. Kyra always goes places."

"BJ, she is with Grandmama. It's a girl's trip," Bryce responded. BJ walked into the house with his head hung low, sad. "You are here with us, and we're going to have fun!" Bryce exclaimed. BJ looked at his daddy with a frown on his face, which made us laugh.

Monday was Bryce's first day at his new job. He kissed me before leaving and said, "I don't know why I'm so nervous, as many times as I've done this."

"Honey, you'll be fine. It's just that you're doing the same job somewhere else," I reassured him.

I finished my morning devotion and walked into the living room, where BJ was lying on the couch watching TV. He had already eaten a bowl of Frosted Flakes and a banana, so I made a simple breakfast for myself. Sitting at the table, I looked out the window and saw a sign that read "MALL" with an arrow pointing in that direction. After finishing my breakfast, BJ and I got dressed and walked to the mall. BJ got excited when he saw a sign for the arcade, so I sent him inside, and I sat my tired self on a bench nearby to watch him play.

Bryce called and asked where we were. "We're at the mall down the street from the Airbnb."

"I'm on the way," he replied. When he found us, I was still sitting on the bench, keeping a watchful eye on BJ. He came over, kissed me, and then went into the arcade to play games with BJ. After about 30 minutes, he came out and said, "I smell food. I'm ready to eat." He helped me up from my seat, and the three of us went to the food court, where they had a soul food restaurant. I ordered a chicken dinner to share with BJ, and Bryce got a roast beef dinner. We sat and ate our food, listening to Bryce tell us about his first day on the job. Our family time was briefly interrupted by Bryce's phone ringing. It was Allen, wanting to know if we wanted to ride to New Hope with him to drop off supplies at the building where the reunion will be held. "Yes, we can ride with you, but we're not at the Airbnb. I'm with Amber and BJ at the mall down the street. Come through Door A. We're sitting in the food court."

When he ended the call, I asked him, "Did you walk here?"

"Yes. I figured if you could walk down here while pregnant, I could, too!" He replied, kissing me on my cheek.

When Allen walked in, he said, "Man, I didn't know all this was in the mall," looking around.

Bryce laughed and replied, "This food is good, too! It tastes like Mama cooked it."

As we walked out, Allen said, "I gotta come back here and get myself some of that food if it tastes like Mama made it!" We all laughed.

On our drive to New Hope, which was about 45 minutes away, Allen told us the schedule for the reunion and mentioned that the park was closed to the public on Saturday. Bryce explained that he would be late on Friday because he didn't get off work until 4:30. "You can wear your uniform to the get-acquainted meeting," Allen suggested.

"I don't like wearing it outside work. I will definitely need time to change," Bryce replied, laughing.

When we reached the building, we all helped Allen bring the supplies inside. He gave us a tour, and then we drove around to see the park. There was a large pavilion, a small lake for swimming, and a playground with all the amenities. It was a nice place to hold a family reunion.

By the time Allen dropped us off at the Airbnb, BJ was asleep, so Bryce carried him inside. I asked, "Are you going to take his clothes off?"

Bryce laughed and said, "He can sleep in his clothes. I'll take off his shoes, though. I don't want him waking up and asking us how the baby is going to get out of your tummy." We laughed about that for a long time. After removing his shoes, Bryce placed his hand on BJ's head, and we prayed before leaving the room.

We walked into our bedroom. I said, "Hon, I'm tired." No sooner than my head hit the pillow, I was asleep.

On Tuesday, Bryce took BJ to work with him. I stayed in bed, finally getting up around 10:00 to make myself some breakfast. I then climbed back into bed and watched TV. Around noon, I received a call from Sherri, who told me she had given birth to her baby two weeks ago and asked how my pregnancy was going. I congratulated her and told her I was doing well, and that I was currently in Alabama with Bryce. "He's on call for his job." We talked for over three hours, laughing about the silly stuff we did growing up. When we hung up, I decided to take a shower before Bryce came in from work. Exiting the shower, I was surprised to see Bryce lying on the bed.

"Hi, Babe. Do you want to go back to the mall to eat dinner? I really enjoyed my meal yesterday," he said. I got dressed quickly, and the three of us went to the mall. After dinner, we went sightseeing around the city. After all that activity, I was tired when we returned to the Airbnb, so I went right to bed, while Bryce and BJ stayed awake, watching TV.

After Bryce left for work on Wednesday, BJ came into my room fully dressed at 10:30, saying he was bored and asking if we could go back to the mall. I got dressed, and we walked there. Once again, I sat on the bench and watched him play in the arcade. Afterward, we went to the food court for lunch. While at the mall, I found a Bath and Body Works store, so I stopped in to pick up gifts to pass out to the ladies at the reunion Friday night. When we returned to the Airbnb, Bryce was in bed, knocked out cold. I didn't wake him. He slept all night without eating dinner. I found out the next morning that the air conditioner had gone out at the job, and the heat had given him a headache.

On Thursday morning, Bryce was up early, cooked breakfast for us all, and we ate together before he left for work. Around 10:00, Rachel called and asked if BJ could come with them to Jayson's soccer game. She added, "Jayson has a tote full of clothes he's outgrown. Would you like them for BJ?"

"Yes, I'd love them. Thank you. BJ will be ready when you get here."

"Okay! See you in about 30 minutes." When she arrived, I was dressed and asked if she could drop me off at Bryce's workplace. He worked on a one-way street, and there was no parking available, so Rachel dropped me off at a four-way stop, which was two buildings away from Bryce's.

As I neared the building, Bryce was stepping out, fanning himself. He looked up and saw me walking toward him. "Amber! Is everything alright? Where is BJ?" he asked frantically.

"Rachel picked him up to go to Jayson's soccer game. I had her drop me off here."

"Come in and meet the other officers. I must warn you: It's hot in there right now," he said, kissing me on the cheek and telling me how beautiful I looked.

After the introductions, the older officer said, "We are closing this building. The repairmen won't be here until next Tuesday to fix the air conditioner. Officer Hollinger, I know tomorrow is your last day here. Fill out these papers, and your assignment is complete. You will be paid for tomorrow, as well as for the two recruits you signed up." He then looked at me and said, "It was nice to meet you, Mrs. Hollinger. Take care of yourself." Bryce signed the papers, shook each man's hand, and we left.

Walking to where the SUV was parked, Bryce said, "I need to change my clothes, and then we'll go get something to eat at the mall. While we're there, we'll look for the frames for the paintings."

While I waited for Bryce to shower and change his clothes, Rachel called, asking if BJ could stay the night with them. "We'll bring him with us to the reunion," she stated.

"Yes," I answered, "but he doesn't have a change of clothes."

"Girl, all these clothes I have here that will fit him!" she replied, laughing hard.

I couldn't help but laugh, especially since she had offered earlier to give me loads of clothes for BJ. "Okay, we'll see you tomorrow."

Bryce called out, "Who are you talking to?"

"It was Rachel. BJ's going to spend the night with them. We'll meet at the reunion tomorrow."

"Great! Okay. Come in here," he said seductively.

I walked into the bedroom and found Bryce lying across the bed in his birthday suit. "Hon, what are you doing?" I asked, shocked. "I thought you were changing your clothes so we could go shopping."

"Shopping can wait," he said, patting a spot on the bed next to him.

A little while later, we drove to the mall and ate at the food court. Afterwards, we walked through the mall looking for a store that sold picture frames. We bought four and then returned to the Airbnb to put the paintings in them. Bryce signed each one 'B. Hollinger and Family.' We went to bed early that night and fell asleep while watching TV.

On Friday morning, Bryce and I woke up early, prayed, had devotion, ate breakfast, and got back into bed. Around 1:30, Kyra called to let us know they were back from the cruise. "Mama, is daddy at work?"

"No, he's here. He can hear you."

"Hi, daddy!"

"Hey, princess! How was your cruise?" he asked.

"Daddy, it was great! I'll tell you all about it on our drive home. Mama, maybe we can go on a cruise someday, just you and me."

"That's something to consider!" I replied.

"Oh! Grandmama wants to know if BJ and I can model tonight."

"Yes, that's fine with us, as long as you're not showing your stomach and thighs," Bryce answered.

"Now, you know Grandmama don't go for that," Kyra said, laughing. "I gotta go. Grandmama is calling for us to get our outfits together. See you guys tonight!"

We arrived at the reunion around 4:30 p.m. Allen greeted us at the door of the venue, saying, "I thought you weren't going to make it until later." Bryce explained what happened at work with the air conditioner. "I'm glad you made it, man."

During the get-acquainted party, Bryce was happy to see many relatives he hadn't seen in years. He took the children and me around to meet everyone. I met his mother's sister, Aunt Lilly, her daughter Natalie, and her two kids. I also met Bryce's uncles. Bryce was surprised to meet his grandfather's oldest son, whom he had never met or seen before. When we all sat down, I looked back and saw Kyra's father. *"What is he doing here?"* I wondered.

When I pointed him out to Bryce, he said, "I met him when I went out to get the paintings. He's just someone who looks like Carl."

"Kyra said he has a beard now. It really looks like him from here," I countered.

Just then, Rachel came over to our table and said the program was about to start. She asked her husband to pray. After the prayer, the Allen girls sang, followed by a poem read by Rachel's daughter titled "What is a Family?" That was followed by Ms. Eva lining up the children for the fashion show. As each child marched around, they gave their name, where they lived, and then stood beside their parents. Allen took pictures of them to include in the family reunion album that would be sent to each head of the family attending. After the fashion show, the gift-giving began. Bryce handed his mother, sister, and brother their framed paintings, and a few others also distributed gifts. I had Kyra give each woman over 18 the gift I bought from Bath and Body Works. The tag on it read, "Family is Everything: From B. Hollinger and Family."

When we lined up for dinner, Kyra brought Zoe and Carlos over, saying, "See, Mama? I told you they were coming to the family reunion." I was surprised and glad to see them at the same time. Although they didn't remember me, I hugged them both. Kyra pulled them away, saying, "Come on. You gotta meet my Grandmama, too!"

It was time to leave once the reunion T-shirts were handed out. As we headed out the door, Ms. Eva, Allen, and Rachel stopped Bryce, telling him they loved their paintings and didn't believe he had painted them until they saw his name. He laughed and said, "It was a family thing," as he hugged them.

On our way back to the Airbnb, I wondered aloud, "Who invited Kyra's father? Who is he related to in your family?"

"Well, Babe," Bryce began, "I pointed him out to Allen. He said that man was Megan's adopted sister's son. Her name is Gail. Megan's mother adopted Gail when she was four after her parents were killed in a car accident."

"I will never forget what Carl did to me, although I'm grateful to have Kyra in my life." We pulled into the garage, and Bryce came around to my side to help me out of the SUV and walk into the house. The whole time, he kissed me and rubbed my belly. "Bryce, what is wrong with you?" I said, giggling.

"You're what's wrong with me. I am infatuated with everything about you," he said before singing in my ear, "I can't get enough of your love, baby." I couldn't help but laugh at his singing.

On Saturday morning, we woke up around 9:00. As Bryce stepped out of the shower, he said, "Babe, do we—"

I cut him off. "No, we don't. Get dressed."

He burst out laughing and replied, "You don't even know what I was going to say!"

"Yes, I do. Now, get dressed."

He came over, kissed me, and said, "I was going to ask if we have enough time to eat breakfast." We both laughed hard at my assumption.

When we arrived at the park, BJ and Kyra were waiting for us. "Mama, y'all are late. What took you so long?" Kyra asked.

"We lost the keys. Thank God, we found them," I replied.

"Daddy, are you going to do the bag race with me?" Kyra asked.

"Yes, but I need to eat first."

"Okay!" she replied happily, walking away. "The race starts in 45 minutes."

"Mama, can I go play dodgeball with Jayson?" BJ asked. I nodded yes, and he ran off to meet up with his cousin.

Bryce and I went to the food tent to get something to eat and drink, then found a seat under the pavilion. "Bryce, is that Carl coming this way?" I asked.

He followed my gaze and said, "He looks like the same guy you pointed out to me last night."

Carl walked up to us and said, "Hey, man. We talked last night. I didn't know you were Amber's husband."

"Yes, she is my better half. The woman the Lord blessed me with," Bryce replied with a big smile on his face.

Carl turned his attention to me. "Amber, I have been thinking about something ever since Kyra visited me. Why didn't you contact me before you let my daughter be adopted and change her last name? I'm considering taking you to court for letting him adopt my daughter without my knowledge."

I looked at Bryce in disbelief, then at Carl. "First of all, Kyra never had your last name. Why would I give my daughter the name of a man who abandoned her before she was born? And when I told you I was pregnant by you, you thought it was a joke. Your friend had to tell you about her. You haven't given her anything except that plane ticket when I sent her to visit you. You saw her once when she was a baby, and again when she was eight at Olivia's memorial service. That was the day you told her you were her daddy. I wish to God you hadn't taken it upon yourself to tell her that, but here we are now. So, Mr. Carl Morgan Benson, I'm giving you my permission to take me to court. Remember, I'm a lawyer, and I know the law. You will lose and have to pay back child support for 14 years—and likely go to jail for what you did to me. Let's not forget that." Bryce just sat there, eating his food and listening to me chew out Carl. Carl stood there, looking like he'd sucked on a lemon.

Kyra broke the tension when she ran up to us and hugged Bryce around his neck. "Daddy, hurry up! They're getting ready to start the race!"

"Okay, princess," he said, rising from his seat before kissing my cheek and walking off with her. Carl watched them with the green eyes of envy as they walked away.

It took everything in me not to yell at that moment and tell everyone what Carl did to me. The only thing that stopped me was when I looked over at my beautiful, healthy daughter, who was full of life, laughing, and enjoying herself with the only daddy she knew. A sense of peace entered my heart, knowing how much I loved her, regardless of the circumstances of her conception. I looked up at Carl and asked, "Is there anything else you want?" with sarcasm dripping from my words.

"No. I'm going to find Zoe now," he replied.

I noticed Bryce looking my way. I gave him a thumbs-up and waved, and he waved back with a smile. "Lord, I thank you for my husband," I murmured.

As I sat there, watching the children play and listening to the hum of conversations around me, a woman approached me, smiling. "I'm Gail. Carl's mother," she said. "Are you Amber?"

"Yes, ma'am. I am."

"Megan tells me your daughter is my granddaughter."

"Yes, she is," I said with a smile.

"Carl never told me he had another daughter," she replied, almost accusingly.

"That's because he never owned up to her."

"She's just as cute as she can be. In fact, she looks like you. You're a beautiful lady," she said, smiling back at me.

"Thank you."

Gail stood there, awkwardly watching me as I ate my cake. I knew she was trying to think of something more to say to me. "Is there anything she needs?" she managed to ask.

"No, ma'am. If you had asked me that same question when she was a baby, I would have had a laundry list of needs. But now, she has everything she needs and more." I smiled and asked if she wanted to join me, but just then, Bryce called my name, telling me to come over or I would miss the race. I stood, and Gail and I moved closer to the bag race starting line to cheer them on.

Shortly after the race began, Gail turned to me and said, "It was nice to meet you, Amber."

I smiled and replied, "It was nice to meet you, too, Ms. Gail." As she walked away, I saw her looking toward Kyra. At 5:00, everyone began cleaning up so we could leave the park by six. As people left, Allen handed out directions to his church, where we would meet for Sunday service the next day.

On our return trip to the Airbnb, Kyra and BJ discussed how much they had enjoyed themselves. Bryce whispered to me, "Where is she going to sleep?"

"You and BJ. Kyra and I," I replied.

"No way! I can't sleep without you in the bed," he said, laughing.

When we walked inside, BJ sat on the couch and said, "I'm going to sleep on the couch. Kyra, you can have my bedroom."

"Thank you, Jesus!" Bryce hollered as he got into bed. He kissed me goodnight and fell asleep minutes later.

On Sunday, we had to be up and dressed to arrive at Allen's church by 11:30. "Be sure to check and make sure you have everything before we leave because once we do, we won't be coming back," Bryce stated.

As we headed to church, Kyra said, "Mama, for about a week, I have been waking up and reading Jeremiah 29:11. Do you remember when you spoke at that women's day program?"

"Yes, I remember."

"Well, I believe the Lord is saying He's going to prosper me when I'm done with school. Grandmama and I are serious about opening a bakery and sandwich shop. We even talked about it on the cruise."

"Kyra, if you submit yourself to God, He will bless you," Bryce confirmed.

"I know, dad. And I thank Him for giving me the best parents and little brother in the world."

"Oh, my goodness. Is this your way of trying to butter us up for something?" Bryce asked.

"No, daddy!" she exclaimed with a chuckle. "I just want y'all to know that I'm changing into a better person. Grandmama said God has great things for me!"

"Indeed, He does. And being obedient is the key."

"I know, dad."

After parking in the church's lot, we entered to find the congregation standing and praying. We waited for the prayer to finish before looking for a seat. Allen saw us and motioned for us to join him up front, next to Ms. Eva.

Once the announcements were read and the deacons finished taking up the offering, the pastor stood and said, "Minister Hollinger called me last night and told me his family was in town and was coming to church with him today. Church, please stand and sing our welcome song to them." They all stood and sang "We Are All a Part of God's Family." Afterward, the pastor said, "Minister Hollinger, it's in your hands."

Allen stood and asked, "Is my sister here?" as he looked out at the congregation. Rachel stood and waved. "I'm sorry. I didn't see y'all. Come up front. I have seats up here for you." Once they were seated, he said, "I thank God for my family coming to our reunion and to church with me today. I pray God's blessings on their trip back to Michigan, Texas, Mississippi, Illinois, New York, and other places. Will all my uncles and their families stand?" They stood and received outstanding applause. When they were seated, Allen continued. "I have my mother here today, and I thank God for her. She is the one who held it all together after our father died, and she didn't let us get away with anything. She kept us in church and on our knees, praying. I witnessed many nights of her praying and baking cakes and pies to help supplement her income just to get us what we needed." He looked over at her and said, "I love you, mom. I wouldn't be the man I am today were it not for you." (I could see her wiping her eyes.) "You all know my beautiful sister, Rachel. She is younger than I am, but she has always had my back. In fact, she had enough confidence in me to follow me here to Montgomery, attend the University, and is now a nurse practitioner. She's here today with her twins and the best brother-in-law I could ever ask for. He is always there when I need him. Thank you, John."

He then looked at Bryce, shaking his head. "And oh, my goodness. Let me tell you about my brother, Bryce. Saints, this handsome man sitting over there had the hardest head as a little boy. He told our Mama everything my sister and I did. There were times when he did something wrong, and he told Mama I did it. And if something were eaten up, he would say Rachel ate it. He would sometimes get into fights and then run home to get me so I could help him. One day, he ran home to ask for my help to fight, but I wasn't home. He got beaten up pretty badly that day. When I arrived, he was sitting on the steps crying, with his clothes hanging off him and dirt and leaves tangled in his hair. He was actually mad at me because I wasn't home to help him! A couple of days later, we went to the park, and he showed me the ones who beat him up. It was three little girls! I asked him why he let those girls beat him up, and he said, 'You told me not to hit girls, so all three of them jumped me at the same time.'" Bryce, along with everyone else, was laughing so hard at the story being told about him. Allen continued, "But today, that hard-headed boy has two years of college with a degree in Political Science under his belt. He has also served in the Navy for 17 years and is now a Senior Recruiting Officer. He's here with his beautiful wife, Amber, who is a lawyer, and their two children, Kyra and BJ, with another on the way. Kyra will bless us with a praise dance shortly." He looked at Bryce and said, "I love you, man. Thank you for looking after our mother." He then asked his wife and children to come up and sing one song.

After the song, he called Kyra to the front. I looked back and saw Carl, his wife, mother, Zoe, and Carlos sitting together on one pew. I thought, *"Every time they call Kyra's name, I know he's thinking about what he is missing and feels bad that she's calling another man daddy."*

Ms. Eva walked up with her, stopping at the microphone to start the music for Kyra. When Kyra reached the front, she said, "I thank God for allowing me to be here today, and I thank Him for Jeremiah 29:11. God tells me every morning when I do my devotion that He has a plan for me." She closed her eyes, prayed, and when she was done, motioned for Ms. Eva to play the "Jeremiah 29:11" song. As she danced, she sang along with it. Her performance was anointed and beautiful. While she danced, the pastor stood, followed by nearly everyone in the church. When she finished, people were running around the church. Some were dancing in the Spirit, while others were speaking in tongues. It was amazing to see God's work in action.

After the Spirit calmed down, the pastor called one of the brothers to come forward and said, "Brother Jesse, look at my sermon. This is what I'm going to preach today. Please read it aloud."

Jesse read, "God's goodness for the children of God. Jeremiah 29:11."

The pastor continued, "Until today, I had never heard that song. God is showing us that He's here today through the praise dance of this child. Mother, please play that song again. I want to listen closely to the words." As the song played again, Kyra continued her praise dance. The pastor ran around the church, and some of the members rejoiced as well. He then preached his sermon and brought the house down!

When the pastor took his seat, one of the deacons stood and announced, "Minister Hollinger just passed me a note. It says, 'Fish is frying in the kitchen. Nobody leaves here hungry today.'" He then blessed the food and dismissed us. People were still rejoicing as we went into the Fellowship Hall.

While everyone was eating, they commented on how much they enjoyed the service. Some were saying their goodbyes and getting their food to go. Rachel came over, hugging me and telling me how much she enjoyed Kyra's praise dance, and to let me know John had put the clothes for BJ in the back of our SUV. "Thank you," I replied, hugging her tightly.

Bryce leaned over and whispered in my ear, "Are you ready to go?"

"Yes, I am. Where are the children?" I asked.

"They're around here somewhere."

Ms. Eva approached us, letting us know she would be staying with her sister for a few weeks before flying home. We let my brother, sister, and a few others know we were leaving, then found the children, who were standing with their cousins. Bryce said to his nieces, "Give us hugs. We're getting ready to leave."

As we were getting into the SUV, Allen came running over with four dinners, handing them to Bryce. "You know Mama is staying with Aunt Lilly for a while, right? I'll be driving her home."

"She told me she's going to fly home," Bryce replied.

Allen burst out laughing. "I'll see you in a few weeks with Mama. You know she's not getting on anybody's plane!"

Just as Bryce opened the door for me to get in, Zoe and Carlos ran up to say goodbye to Kyra. She stepped out and hugged them. Carl walked up behind them and asked if he could talk with us before we left. "Yes," Bryce answered. Kyra stood there, listening to the conversation. Carl asked us to forgive him for what he said about Kyra.

"What did you say about me?" Kyra asked.

"Kyra, get in the SUV," Bryce instructed.

She began to cry, saying, "Daddy, please don't send me back to his house."

"Kyra, you're not going anywhere but home with us," I said.

Carl stood there, looking sad, and said, "I'm sorry. I really am."

Bryce approached him. "Man, we forgive you. Take care of yourself." He fist-bumped Carl and signaled for me to get in the SUV. Carl stood where he was, watching us drive away.

Kyra was in the backseat, crying. "Mama, why was he talking about me?"

"Kyra, stop crying. We talked to him at the park. He said something to your daddy and me, and he wanted to apologize."

"I don't have to go with him?" she asked.

"No, you don't have to go with him," I replied. Fifteen minutes later, I glanced back, and both of them were asleep, with BJ resting his head on Kyra's shoulder. I took my phone out of my purse and took a picture of them.

We stopped for gas and a bathroom break in Delhi, Louisiana, and ate the food Allen gave us. Once we got back on the road, the kids were wide awake, and Kyra told us more about her cruise and the shopping she did with her Grandmama. Before we knew it, we were crossing the Texas state line. We made it home around midnight.

Later that morning, Bryce and BJ went to check on Ms. Eva's dog after agreeing to take care of it while she was away. I relaxed on the patio in the backyard, appreciating the wooden fence Bryce had the men install, and said aloud, "There's no place like home." I started thinking about the week ahead, grateful that I didn't have to go back to work, with Bryce off until Monday. With the children heading back to school soon, I needed to start planning for the baby. I was getting more and more excited about the future. My quiet time was interrupted when Kyra came into my room to tell me her daddy was bringing home pizza and asked if I wanted anything else. "Please tell him to bring a salad from Subway," I responded. When Bryce and BJ got home, Bryce told me that when the dog saw BJ, it jumped all over him. He had me laughing so hard about that dog that my sides were hurting.

On Friday, Kyra and I went shopping. We bought some things for the baby, school supplies for her and BJ, and items for their get-together on Saturday. Bryce had told them they could have some friends over for a pool party before they head back to school.

On Saturday morning, Kyra and BJ were up early, cleaning around the pool and hanging decorations. For snacks, we ordered Subway sandwiches that were cut into small pieces with a toothpick holding them together, chips, cookies that Kyra baked, and punch. By 3:00 p.m., all their guests had arrived. They played games, swam, and danced around the pool.

"This was the best get-together ever!" Kyra said after everyone left. BJ nodded in agreement.

Three weeks had gone by, and Bryce hadn't heard from his Mama. He called her phone, only for it to go straight to voicemail. He then FaceTimed Allen, asking him about their mother. "She said she lost her phone and that all her numbers are in it," Allen reported.

"I found a phone in the SUV. It's probably hers," Bryce replied.

Allen laughed and said, "I will tell Mama to stop looking and that you have it. I'm glad you called because she thought she lost it on the cruise ship. Listen, I'll bring her home on Saturday. We should be there around 4:00 p.m. My son, AJ, is coming with me to help with the driving. We'll spend the night at Mama's house and leave around 4:00 a.m. Sunday morning."

"Thanks, big bro."

While they were still talking, my Mama called. I mouthed to Bryce, letting him know who it was, and left the room to speak to her. She called to let me know that Brandon had reached out to her, asking to pray that his request to move back to the States be granted. Before hanging up, she said, "I'm looking forward to seeing you in a few weeks!"

I sat there, thinking about my handsome brother. I remembered the time he signed up for a Michael Jackson singing contest. He practiced every day, sliding across the floor, dancing, and standing in front of the mirror, singing "I'm Bad," "Man in the Mirror," and "Billie Jean." As the day of the contest neared, he got a Jheri Curl and an outfit that matched the music superstar's, complete with a sequined glove. He bought me and my friend Phillis outfits that looked like his because we were his backup dancers. (Phillis was Jay's sister.)

On the night of the contest, we thought we'd be home before Mama got in from the salon. We weren't. Many contestants had signed up to perform, and we were next to the last ones to be called. When it was our turn, Brandon rocked the stage when he sang "Man in the Mirror." He tied with another boy, so they had to sing a tie-breaking song. Brandon sang "Billie Jean," and won first place. His prize was $900.00. He gave Phillis and me $150.00 each.

After we dropped Phillis off at home, Brandon said, "I hope Mama is asleep. It's already 1:30 a.m. I didn't know we'd be so far down the list." He pulled into the driveway and immediately saw that the house was dark. We tried to slip inside unnoticed, but as soon as Brandon closed the door, Mama flipped on the lights, causing us to jump.

She was furious and yelled at Brandon first. "You got this girl out there shaking her behind in those tight clothes, and I'm sitting here worrying about y'all! Don't you ever do that again! Do you hear me, boy?"

Brandon tried to stop her from yelling. "Mama! Mama! We won first place," he said, showing her the money and placing a $100.00 bill in her hand.

She paused, looked at the money, and said, "Thank you."

Then, she started in on me. "I better not ever hear of you on a stage shaking your behind again! Now, get out of here," she yelled at both of us.

On Sunday morning, she made us get up early for church. When we walked in, I saw Phillis sitting on the back pew near the wall. Brandon and I sat beside her. She said, "Girl, my mom was so mad at me when I got home. She said if she ever hears of me out there dancing again wearing those little, skinny pants, she will put me out of her house!" We laughed so hard. I then told her what Mama said to me, and we giggled all through the service. All I can say is that we never danced that way again.

Nine months later, Brandon left for an Undercover Secret Service International Training course. When he returned home, I was pregnant and preparing to graduate from high school. He stayed with us for a month before receiving a call to go on an undercover mission in the United Kingdom.

My thoughts were interrupted when Bryce came into the family room and asked, "Is your mom alright?"

"Yes, she's fine. She was just telling me that Brandon called her."

"Is he alright?" he asked, concerned. I told him about the conversation and finished by saying that she'd arrive before the baby is born. "That's good news. Well, Mama will be home on Saturday. She can take care of her own dog. She says she's keeping it for BJ, but I think she's keeping that dog for herself," he said, chuckling. "BJ said he liked playing with the dog, but he doesn't like cleaning up behind him. You need to see his face when he's picking up that poop!" At that point, Bryce was cracking up.

"Do you help him at all?" I asked.

"No, I don't. I sit on the patio and watch him do it himself." While we were talking and laughing about BJ's chore, he came outside. "Are you ready to go and clean up after the dog?" Bryce asked, still laughing.

The look on BJ's face said it all. "Oh, man!" he whined.

The days kept passing quickly. One Friday night, the four of us gathered in the family room to pick a name for the baby. By that time, we knew we were having a boy. The name we chose was Eric Cornelius. Eric was Bryce's dad's name, and Cornelius was my father's name.

That Saturday afternoon, Allen called to let us know they were at their mom's house. Bryce invited them over for dinner. When they arrived, Allen carried in a tote full of baby gifts. We all sat around the table, ate, and enjoyed each other's company. Around 8:00 p.m., they prepared to leave to get some rest before their return trip in the morning.

Ms. Eva hugged Bryce and said, "Thank you, Baby Boy, for looking after the dog for me."

He laughed and asked, "Mama, are you sure that's BJ's dog, or is he your dog?"

She looked at BJ, winked, and replied, "It's our dog. Right, BJ?" He just smiled, making all of us laugh at his expression.

On Wednesday, Ms. Eva called early in the morning and asked if Kyra could come over after school. She needed help to bake ten cakes and six dozen cookies by the weekend. "Yes, she can come, as long as she does her homework while she's there," I said.

She laughed and replied, "She already knows, she doesn't do anything here until that homework is finished!"

After Bryce left for work and the children went to school, I spent the entire day sorting through the baby clothes. Combining the tote Allen bought with the items we already purchased, the baby had everything he needed. My job provided us with gift cards, and the officers who worked with Bryce gave us enough diapers and wipes to last six months or more. Some members of our church also sent gifts.

Monday afternoon, Bryce asked, "When is the baby due?"

"In four weeks or less," I answered.

"Babe, I have a job assignment in Ohio the second week of September."

"Ohio?!"

"Yes, in Fairfield, not far from Cincinnati. I should be back before the baby arrives."

"I thought you were going on paternity leave once we got back from the reunion, Bryce," I replied, clearly unhappy.

"My leave starts the weekend that I get back from Ohio. That will be two weeks before the baby is due," he explained.

I got up and went into my mom's room to finish the butterflies painting I was working on that would be hung in her room. I was so disappointed that Bryce had to leave so close to the time the baby was due to arrive. A little while later, Bryce came in, took the paintbrush from my hand, and hugged me, saying, "Let's go out and get something to eat from Red Lobster. When we return, we'll finish this painting together."

"Are you taking me out just because you're leaving?" I asked.

He laughed and said, "Well, I don't smell anything cooking on the stove, and I'm hungry. I'm sure Eric is hungry, too." On our way out, Kyra called, asking if she could run for homecoming queen. We both said it was okay with us. She sounded excited as she hung up the phone. When we returned home, as promised, Bryce worked on the painting with me until we both got sleepy. I told him I'd have it finished by the time he made it back from Ohio.

Sunday afternoon, Bryce flew out for his job in Ohio. Later that week, as the children ate their breakfast before leaving to catch the school bus, Kyra asked, "What are we doing for daddy's birthday on Saturday?"

"We'll go shopping when you get home from school," I replied, hugging them as they walked out the door. When they got home, we went to the mall. Although they had their own money, I gave each of them $20.00. While at JCPenney's, I bought the Nike outfit I had heard Bryce say he wanted, Kyra got him an Oak and Luma beaded bracelet, and BJ picked out a Nike cap and socks that matched the outfit I chose. We also stopped at Dollar Tree for the decorations. On the way home, we picked up dinner from Arby's.

We ate our food and then wrapped the gifts. Afterwards, I sat back and watched the children decorate the family room for their daddy's birthday celebration. When they finished, we prayed and went to bed.

On Friday morning, Kyra got up early and made us breakfast, explaining that she was hungry when she woke up. After they boarded the bus, I prayed, then read Psalm 91 and Isaiah 40. As I sat there, reflecting on those scriptures in my heart, Ms. Eva called to check on me. I told her what I read for my devotion that morning, and she said, "I read Psalm 91 this morning as well. I believe God is letting us know that whatever we go through, He'll be there to protect us."

"Thank you for your words of encouragement, Ms. Eva. Since I have you on the phone... Tomorrow is Bryce's birthday. I'm planning to have dinner ready for him when he gets home."

"What time will he arrive?" she asked.

"His plane lands at 2:30. He should be home around 4:30."

"How about this? I'll come over around 1:00 and cook dinner for you. Kyra can bake a cake. Just have everything needed when I get there." Then I heard her say, "What's that dog barking at now? Oh. Amber, it's Mrs. Dickenson, coming to pick up her pies. Hold those scriptures close to your heart, and remember that God is our protector," she said before ending the call.

I went into Mama's room, determined to finish the painting while meditating on the scriptures. Thirty minutes later, it was completed, and it looked beautiful. I framed it and hung it on the wall by the window so Mama would see it as soon as she entered the room. Then I went to my room and fell asleep. When I woke up, it was past 1:00, and I still needed to run to the store to get the supplies Ms. Eva needed to prepare Bryce's dinner. I wanted to be back home before the children arrived. On the way to the store, the traffic was unusually heavy for 2:00 in the afternoon. I was stopped at a red light, and when it turned green, I started to go. The last thing I remember was hearing my car being hit and the airbags deploying.

When I regained consciousness, I was in the hospital. Bryce was at my bedside, holding my hand with his head bowed, still in his uniform. I didn't know whether he was praying or sleeping. I moved my hand slightly to get his attention. He lifted his head, kissed me, and said, "You're awake. Thank you, Lord! You are alright."

Instinctively, my hand moved to my belly. I rubbed it and immediately noticed it was no longer swollen. "Where's my baby?" I asked frantically.

"He's in the nursery. He's fine," Bryce said, looking at me with concern. "Do you know what happened?"

"Vaguely. What day is it?" I asked.

"It's Saturday afternoon."

"What? Saturday afternoon?" I had been unconscious for over 24 hours!

He nodded slowly. "I was on my way to the airport when Terry called, saying D'Ericka had called him to let him know you were in a car accident and were unconscious. D'Ericka was working in the emergency room when they brought you and the other driver in. I called my Mama, told her what happened, and asked her to go to our house to wait for the children to get home from school. When I got here, you were unconscious, but all your and the baby's vital signs were good. I received a call from the officer investigating the accident, who found your purse and phone in the SUV, asking me to come and identify your belongings. Amber, when I saw that SUV, I knew it was the Lord who blessed you to come out alive. The other car was badly damaged, too. Around 3:00 this morning, the baby's heart rate began to drop, so they did an emergency C-section. He is a beautiful baby, with a head full of black hair, and looks like BJ when he was born."

"Bryce, I need to see our baby." He called for the nurse to bring in Eric. When I saw him, he was perfect. Bryce asked the nurse to take a picture of us. He weighed 7 lbs. 12 oz., born on his father's birthday: September 16th at 3:20 a.m. I looked at Bryce lovingly and said, "Happy birthday, honey. Eric Cornelius Hollinger is your special gift." I told him to go home and get some rest. I knew he was tired.

After he left, I lay there, looking at my baby and thanking God for saving us from that accident. I also thought about what Ms. Eva said regarding God being my protector and how God had protected baby Eric and me when I was kidnapped by that man. I started to cry, thanking the Lord for saving our lives. A short time later, a nurse brought in my food and took Eric back to the nursery to put him under the light to prevent him from contracting jaundice. After eating, I closed my eyes, rested, and continued to thank God for saving my life.

My rest was disturbed by a soft knock on the door. A young man slowly opened it. He was in a wheelchair with one arm in a sling, a cast on one leg, and a bandage around his head. "Who are you looking for?" I asked.

"Are you Mrs. Hollinger?"

"Yes, I am."

"Ma'am, I asked the nurse which room you were in. I'm the person who caused the accident. I just wanted to see if you're okay. I'm so sorry," he said.

"I forgive you, young man. It was an accident, and we're both alive. Thank God."

"Ma'am, you might not recognize me, but I know who you are. You're the lawyer who kept my friend and me out of prison. Do you remember the fire case? They thought my friend and I started it."

"Yes, I remember the case well."

"Thank you for helping us in court. I'm so glad I didn't kill you," he said, trying his best to smile through the pain.

"Give all credit to God. It was He who kept you out of prison, and it was He who spared our lives in that accident. What's your name, young man?" I asked.

"Grant Smith," he answered.

"Thank you, Grant, for coming to check on me."

He nodded and turned to roll his way back out the door, just as a nurse was coming in with baby Eric. Grant stopped and exclaimed, "You were pregnant!"

"Yes, I was."

"Oh, my God! I hit you, and you were pregnant? I'm so sorry," he said apologetically as he closed the door behind him.

Bryce called to let me know that my Mama would come to the hospital as soon as she returned from her trip. We talked for a few minutes before I told him I had to go because the nurse was ready to see if I could nurse Eric. "I love you," he said, and then hung up the phone.

Monday morning, I was up early to bottle-feed Eric. After feeding him, a nurse took him back to the nursery. I got up, took a shower, and was walking around the room when Bryce came in around 9:30. He said, "My Mama will bring the children up when they get home from school. They have a half-day today and tomorrow." A little while later, a nurse brought the baby back in, and Bryce sat beside me in the recliner, bottle-feeding him.

Once again, Grant knocked on the door and slowly entered. When Bryce saw him, he asked, "Weren't you at the recruiting office on Center and Addison a couple of weeks ago?"

"Yes, sir. I'm supposed to leave for training in San Antonio next month. Can I still go if I've been in a car accident?" he asked with concern.

"You'll need to contact your recruiting officer. He'll let you know," Bryce replied.

Grant sat in the wheelchair, watching Bryce feed Eric. "Sir, I'm Grant. I'm the one who hit your wife's SUV. I'm so sorry."

"I know who you are, young man. She told me you came in yesterday and apologized."

"Your wife wasn't upset with me for causing the accident. In fact, she told me to thank God for delivering us from it. How can I thank someone I can't see?" he asked. Bryce and I talked to him about God and salvation. Grant gave his life to the Lord that night, saying, "I knew He brought me out of that accident for a reason." Bryce told him to read his Bible and even invited him to our church.

While they were talking, the door slowly opened. Ms. Eva and the children walked in. When BJ saw Grant, he asked, "What happened to you, Grant?"

"I was in an accident," Grant answered.

"How do you know him, BJ?" Bryce asked, surprised.

"He worked at my summer camp," BJ said, smiling. Grant explained that he was working for summer credits while finishing his second year in college. He also mentioned that he had enlisted in the Air Force so he could complete his degree for free. As he spoke, he kept glancing at Kyra, who was sitting next to Ms. Eva with baby Eric.

Bryce followed Grant's glance. "Do you know her?" he asked.

"No, sir. But I'd like to," he answered sincerely.

"Well, she's my daughter. And no, she's not dating. Now, you can roll yourself on out of here."

Grant laughed hard and said, "Thank y'all for explaining the Bible to me." He turned, fist-bumped BJ, and then locked eyes with Kyra.

"Boy, roll out of here and read your Bible. Start with Proverbs and pray," Bryce said, laughing. Ms. Eva sat there, shaking her head at him as he rolled out of the room.

Four days later, baby Eric and I were discharged from the hospital. When I walked through the door, carrying Eric, Mama came out of the family room. I was glad to see her, and she was excited to meet her new grandson. I told her his name, and she said, "If your daddy were here, he would be honored to have a grandson named after him." She held him close, whispering, "Eric Cornelius Hollinger. That's such a wonderful name."

Mama stayed with us for three months before returning to Virginia. I began missing her the moment she walked out the door. I would go into her room every morning to do my devotion for a couple of months after she left. When Eric was four months old, Bryce and I picked up my new SUV. It was a Chevrolet Traverse, just like the one that had been totaled, but it was light gray instead of black. When Eric was five months old, I was called to return to work on a case I had been waiting over a year to get a trial date for. Eric was placed in a daycare down the street from our house, and Bryce or Kyra picked him up on the days I ran late at work.

One day, while I was at work, Bryce called me. "What are you doing?" he asked.

"Just sitting here, reading over a case."

"Come outside. I want you to go somewhere with me," he teased. "I'm pulling up to your building now." I grabbed my purse and told my secretary I was leaving. By the time I made it outside, Bryce was there, already waiting for me.

Once I was settled in the passenger's seat and had secured my seatbelt, I asked, "Where are we going?"

"I have something to show you."

"Do you want me to close my eyes?"

"No, that's not necessary," he said, laughing.

We drove past the street where we lived and then turned at a red light four blocks down into the mall. "We're getting something at the mall?" I asked, confused.

"No. We're meeting a man to show us that building over there," he replied, pointing to a building under renovation.

"What are you going to do with a building?" I asked, my voice rising with each word.

He grinned slyly and said, "It's Mama and Kyra's bakery! The men we're going to meet are here already." We parked, stepped out of the car, and approached two men. Bryce spoke first. "Hello. I'm Bryce Hollinger, and this is my wife, Amber. I spoke to one of you earlier today."

An average-sized Asian man stepped forward and extended his hand. "Hi, Bryce. I'm the one you spoke with. I'm Leo Chung, and this is my brother, Eugene," he said as he shook

Bryce's and my hands. He then opened the door and held it for us as we entered.

The building's interior was more spacious than it looked from the outside. Leaning against one wall was a tall mirror and broken pieces of plywood. Drywall, empty boxes, and other trash were scattered all over the floor, everywhere we looked. Although no one was working inside, it was clear that renovations were underway. In the front room, there was a display case. That room led to a smaller one with a desk that connected to the kitchen. In the kitchen, there were two industrial-sized stoves, three ovens, a large refrigerator, a chest deep freezer, and a long table stacked with pots, pans, and other cooking utensils. Down the hallway were two bathrooms, and at the end was an apartment with a living room, a small room on one side, a bathroom, and a big bedroom with a large closet with mirror doors. The entire building needed to be repainted, and new carpeting needed to be installed throughout, but I could see the potential. I could tell by the expression on Bryce's face that he was happy with what he saw.

Leo told us that his mother started renovating the building for a bakery and planned to sell her house and move into the apartment. Sadly, she caught COVID and was hospitalized for three weeks before passing away from the disease. He lives in Washington, DC, and his brother lives in Detroit, Michigan. They had been in the area for two months trying to sell the property. The week before, they sold her house and car and were eager to sell the bakery so they could return to their families.

Bryce extended his condolences and then said, "I like the building, but you're asking a lot for it, and a lot of work needs to be done."

Leo asked to be excused and then pulled his brother aside. When they returned, he said they had agreed to lower the price to $250,000.00, to be purchased as-is. Eugene showed us the papers detailing the work that had already been completed inside.

After a moment of contemplative silence, Bryce asked, "So, how do you guys want to do this?" Leo stated that they would need a deposit, and then they would immediately take it off the market. Bryce and I agreed, and we went to the bank. We returned with a cashier's check for $10,000.00 and signed a promissory note, stating that we would have the balance on Friday at 3:00 p.m.

"Thank you," Leo said, taking the check, folding it, and then tucking it into his suit jacket pocket. "I will revise the deed to reflect the updated selling price and have it ready for your signatures when we meet back here on Friday," Leo stated. We all shook hands before parting ways.

As Bryce and I approached our house, I glanced at the cameras and saw Kyra and BJ heading to the daycare to pick up Eric. When they returned, Kyra shouted, "Daddy, what are you doing home?"

"I got off early. Your Mama is in here, too," he yelled back to her from the bedroom.

"Where's her ride?"

"At work. I picked her up early because we had some business to handle."

"May I come in and give you Eric?" Kyra asked.

"Yes, you can," I replied. When she handed Eric to Bryce, she said that the daycare director needed more diapers and wipes, and that his empty bottles were in his diaper bag. "Okay. Please put the empty bottles in the kitchen sink."

Bryce asked, "Where is BJ?"

"He's outside, talking to his friend. Daddy, I'm working on my campaign speech on why I should be the homecoming queen."

"And how's that going?" he asked.

"It's going well. A lot of the students said they would vote for me! And daddy, this boy at school is always looking at me."

"Maybe he likes you. Just tell him you don't date, then invite him to church."

She laughed and said, "Daddy, I can't say that to him! But he is cute!" As she walked out the door, she stopped and asked, "Mama, what's for dinner?"

"Leftovers."

"Again?" she said with a loud sigh.

Bryce chuckled at her response. "She's just joking. I'm going out to get pizza in a little while." That brought a smile to Kyra's face as she left. He then said to me, "Our little girl is growing up, and some little boy is looking at her. I'm not ready for that yet." As he sat in the recliner, playing with Eric, he was smiling from ear to ear when he said, "I know Mama is going to love that building. I can see the sign now: 'Eva and Kyra's Bakery and Sandwich Shop—with Hand-Dipped Ice Cream.'"

"I don't remember either of them saying anything about ice cream, Bryce!"

"That will be for BJ. He just doesn't know it yet. It's not a lot of work to do, and he won't feel left out," he said with a broad smile. "Babe, call the kids. I don't want pizza. We're going out to dinner to celebrate the new building. Don't tell them yet, though, because they'll tell Mama," he said, laughing.

When we got back home from dinner, we had family time and did a Bible study, and then the children disappeared to their rooms. I breast-fed Eric and laid him down in his crib. I took a quick shower and got into bed. When Bryce came to bed, he leaned over and asked, "Are you asleep?"

"A little bit," I replied sleepily.

He laughed and asked, "How can anybody be a little bit asleep?"

"Okay. I'm awake. What do you want, Hon?"

He kissed me on the cheek and said excitedly, "I'm ready to talk about the building!"

"Go to sleep, Bryce," I replied, turning over and drifting off to sleep.

On Friday, we finalized the building purchase as planned. Bryce was so happy after signing the papers that he spent that afternoon gathering trash into bags. On Saturday, he woke up early, waiting at the site for the commercial-sized dumpster to arrive. His afternoons and Saturdays were spent at the building removing debris from inside and tossing it into the dumpster.

In October, Kyra was crowned homecoming queen. On the night of the homecoming, we left Eric at Ms. Eva's and headed to the field to watch her ride on the float. Queen Kyra looked beautiful! That evening, her school's football team played against Northeastern High, and her school came out on top. The young man who won homecoming king approached us and introduced himself as Kendrick. He was a handsome, tall, and very polite young man.

On Saturday morning, we all slept in late. Kyra and BJ cooked breakfast, which Bryce ate before heading out to work on the building. BJ asked, "Daddy, where do you go every Saturday?"

"I'm doing a clean-up job in a building," he replied.

"Can I come?"

"Not today, son. But one day, you can come and sweep for me." That seemed to satisfy BJ.

Allen, Rachel, and their families came to visit for Thanksgiving. Allen's family stayed at our house, and Rachel's family stayed at their Mama's house. We all spent Thanksgiving Day at our house. After dinner, we played games while multiple conversations took place throughout the room.

Friday morning, all of us ladies went shopping for the Black Friday sales, leaving the men and boys at home with baby

Eric. That afternoon, when we returned, we all went to see the movie "Forge," and everyone enjoyed it.

Early Saturday morning, Allen, Rachel, and their families left to return to Montgomery. While Bryce and I relaxed in our bedroom, watching TV, Kyra came in and said, "I need to talk."

"About what?" I asked.

"Zoe's grandmother, Gail, called me. She said she wanted me to visit her for Christmas, and now that she knows I'm her granddaughter, she wants to get to know me better."

"When did she call and tell you that?"

"A few minutes ago. Zoe gave her my number."

"And what did you tell her?" Bryce asked.

"I told her I was spending Christmas with my family, and she said, 'I'm your family, too. Zoe is coming here for Christmas, and if you come, I'll have both of my granddaughters here with me.' I told her I was sorry, but I couldn't come."

"Kyra, she just wants to spend some time with you," I said gently.

She yelled, "Daddy, don't let Mama send me to that lady's house! Please!"

"I'm not sending you anywhere you don't want to go, Kyra," I replied. "I was just saying that she wants to spend some time with you."

"Well, then, you go and spend time with her! I'm not going anywhere!" she shouted.

Bryce looked at her, surprised. "Kyra! Don't you dare speak to your Mama in that tone of voice!" He quickly calmed down and said, "Whenever you want to go for a visit, it will be your choice."

"I'm sorry, Mama," she said sincerely. "You don't know how I felt when you sent me to those strange people's house and had to walk through that big airport with people staring at me. It was torture!" She locked eyes with me and said, "Whenever you want to put me out again, just send me to Grandmama's house." The way she said it was so funny, we all burst out laughing loud and hard. After our laughter died down, she asked if we wanted to see the painting she and BJ finished.

"Yes, let's see what it looks like," I replied. She ran out of the room to grab the painting. BJ was with her when she returned. "That's beautiful!" Bryce nodded in agreement.

"Mama, where are you going to hang it?" BJ asked.

"We will find somewhere special for it after we get it framed," Bryce answered.

Before we knew it, Christmas was just around the corner. A week before the holiday, Bryce and BJ put up decorations and strung lights all around the house. We spent one night as a family decorating a huge tree in the family room window. Later that week, Kyra was busy helping Ms. Eva bake her Christmas orders. I stopped by her house one afternoon on my way home from work to pick up Eric from daycare, and I took pictures of Ms. Eva and Kyra working in the kitchen. I noticed how small the space they were working in was and thought, "They're really going to love that building!" Ms. Eva's business was growing, especially during the holiday season.

When I got home, I laid Eric on Kyra's bed and then looked for the recipes she had made for her cookbook. I was impressed by how neatly she kept her room. I finally spotted the small pile of recipes on her dresser, each labeled with step-by-step instructions on how to make them, along with pictures of the cookies and cakes she planned to include. I took a picture of each page, knowing the published cookie cookbook was going to be great. I heard Bryce calling my name, so I hurried to put everything back as Kyra had left it. I picked up Eric and left the room.

"What are you doing?" Bryce asked as he kissed me and took Eric from my arms.

"Just admiring how neatly Kyra is keeping her room."

He looked around and said, "It's funny. The sign she put up in each officer's office is still there. Mine is, too. I guess everyone's afraid to take it down." We both laughed. "Where's BJ?"

"At your mom's house. I stopped by on my way home, and he said he wanted to stay. You know, your mom is going to appreciate the space in that building. She had cakes, cookies, and pies everywhere!"

"I have a catering job for her if she wants to do it. All four military branches are coming together for our New Year's Eve party. The pay is good," he said, winking at me.

On Christmas Eve, Ms. Eva spent the night with us. "We baked 58 cakes, 45 dozen Christmas cookies, 35 pies, and 35 dozen homemade rolls. I am ready for a break!" she exclaimed as she went into the guest room, turned on the TV, and got into bed.

On Christmas morning, we had our devotion and then worked together to prepare a big Christmas breakfast. Afterward, we sang Christmas carols, and Bryce told the Christmas story. Then, we opened our gifts. We bought Ms. Eva a red sweater dress and gave her a $75.00 Visa gift card. She also opened the gifts Allen and Rachel left for her when they visited for Thanksgiving. Bryce received a briefcase, a sweater, and cologne. Ms. Eva had gifts for all of us, too. Kyra got a new phone, BJ a new game, and baby Eric a push toy. Bryce and I also bought a couple of new games for the family, which we played throughout the day, between meals. When night fell, we loaded into the SUV and drove around town to look at the Christmas lights.

Later, when we dropped Ms. Eva off at her house, Bryce asked if she wanted to cater for the party on New Year's Eve and shared the details. "Yes, I would love to do it!" she said happily.

"And, Grandmama, I can help you get everything together!" Kyra offered.

"Yes, I will need your help, Kyra." That weekend, they decorated the building together, and on Monday, they prepared the food for the event. On New Year's Eve, we arrived at 7:00 p.m. Ms. Eva was already there and had everything looking so nice. Bryce was impressed by how his mom had transformed the place. She had each branch of service decorated in their colors. "Thank you all for my Christmas gift card. I spent it on jewelry. How do you like it?" she asked, modeling her pieces. We told her how amazing both she and the decorations looked. "I couldn't have gotten it down without Kyra. I'm going to pay her for helping me."

Around 8:00, people began to arrive, commenting on how beautifully the place was decorated and how good the food table looked. Thankfully, I took pictures of the food table before everyone started to eat. Bryce and I don't drink alcohol, but we enjoyed the music and dancing together throughout the night. Ms. Eva left around 10:00, and we didn't get home until well after midnight. Kyra was asleep in our bed, and Eric was asleep in his. That night, we slept in the guest bedroom because we didn't want to wake them.

The next day, Bryce got dressed and said he was going to meet his mom at the building to help her pack up her belongings. Around 11:00, he called me to let me know that his mom had received orders from some of the partygoers to make four dozen rolls, three coconut Italian cakes, and three dozen cookies for Saturday. She was thrilled!

After hanging up the call, I browsed through my phone and selected the pictures I wanted to add to Kyra's cookbook. I didn't want to alter anything she already had; I just wanted to include a few of the photos I had taken. I had my choices printed, grabbed Kyra's manuscript, and, when I arrived at work on Thursday, asked my secretary, London, to place the new photos where they belonged in the book. I also shared our plans to surprise Kyra with the published book during her birthday party.

"I don't want to miss that," London said. "I'll organize everything in the book and fix the spelling if needed."

That afternoon, as I turned onto my street, I saw Kyra walking with baby Eric toward the house. I reflected on how helpful she'd been with BJ and Eric and was happy to be working on her book. We reached the garage at the same time, so I opened it to pull in. Kyra waited for me to get out, but BJ ran past, saying he "had to use it." Once inside, Kyra set the baby in his walker and asked, "What's for dinner?"

"I'm baking a chicken and making mac-and-cheese, green beans, and cornbread muffins."

"That sounds good!" she said, heading to her room. A few minutes later, she came back and said, "Mama, I meant to ask: Did you or my daddy go into my room?"

I paused cleaning the chicken and asked, "Go into your room?" I wondered how she knew.

"When I was at Grandmama's house, somebody went into my room. BJ knows he's not allowed in my room without permission, so I'm thinking it was either you or daddy."

Bryce walked into the kitchen just then and asked, "What are my two favorite ladies talking about?" as he kissed my cheek.

"Daddy, did you go into my room?" Kyra asked. He rubbed his head, as if trying to recall whether he had entered her bedroom or not.

"Well, Eric and I walk through every room in the house and pray," I said.

"I could tell somebody has been in my room because my rug was messed up, and my pens and jewelry weren't in the same position I left them," Kyra said accusingly.

"I didn't touch your pencils. Nor did I walk on your rug," I replied, trying to hold back my laughter. She explained how she kept a specific spot for her pens and jewelry on her dresser, and that when she came home, they were scattered everywhere. While she talked, Bryce left the kitchen, cracking up because he knew I had been snooping in her room. "Maybe when I stood the baby on your dresser, his foot hit your pens." She giggled, shook her head, and went back to her room. I put the chicken in the oven, picked up Eric from his walker, and went into my bedroom. I collapsed onto the bed, laughing until my stomach hurt.

On January 15th, the children had the day off from school for Martin Luther King, Jr. Day, so we went to the circus. When we left, we stopped by Ms. Eva's for a visit while Bryce fixed her bedroom door. The Saturday before my birthday, Sherri called, saying they were in town for Kelvin's uncle's memorial service and asked if they could stop by to see us. "Yes! We'd love to see you," I replied, giving her our address.

Around 4:30, Sherri and her family arrived. "Come on in, guys. Have a seat." I then introduced them to the children.

Sherri said, "Oh, my God! Kyra, you are the spitting image of your mom. I was at the hospital when you were born." Kyra smiled. She then introduced her children to us. The oldest was named Kelvin, Jr., the little girl was Shyra, and her baby boy, who was a month older than Eric, was named Avory.

When Bryce came in from working at the bakery, I introduced them. "This is my husband, Bryce. Bryce, this is my best friend, Sherri, and her husband, Kelvin."

Bryce shook their hand and said, "So, you're the friend Amber is always talking about."

"All good things, I hope," Sherri said, laughing. "Amber, you have a beautiful home."

"Thank you. Let me show you around."

When we entered Mama's room, Sherri said, "Amber, it's beautiful back here. So many butterflies!"

"Yes, you know Mama loves her butterflies. If she had stayed here with me, she planned to have that window removed and replaced with a patio door, and to plant a flower and vegetable garden out back. What time are you flying out tonight?" I asked.

"We're not leaving until tomorrow afternoon. Once we leave here, we're heading to a hotel near the airport."

"Why don't y'all stay here tonight, then?" I asked.

"I'll see what Kelvin thinks about that. Girl, your husband is a good-looking man. Where did you meet him?" she asked, giggling. I told her the story about the day we met at church. "For real, Amber?"

"Yes, for real. God sent him to me. He's a good man and loves Kyra like she's his own daughter. Girl, she will ask him for something before asking me. As a matter of fact, she thought he was her father until we went to a memorial service, and Carl was there. That man told her he was her daddy."

Sherri's jaw dropped open. "No, he didn't!"

"Yes, he did. Then, we went to a family reunion last summer, and guess who was there? Carl! I found out my sister-in-law's mother had adopted Carl's mother when she was three or four. Her name is Gail."

"Wait. Are you talking about Gail Johnson?"

"No, Sherri," I said, laughing. "Think about it. Gail Johnson was the same age as us!"

Bryce and Kelvin joined us in Mama's room. Bryce was laughing hysterically and said, "Amber, this guy right here has had me cracking up ever since he's been here!"

"Oh, my goodness. Have you been telling your jokes again, Kelvin?" Sherri asked, chuckling.

Bryce took Eric out of my arms and sat on the stool beside me. "He preached to me first, and then he told me some jokes."

Kelvin sat on the couch beside Sherri and their baby. "Kelvin, Amber invited us to stay here tonight so that we don't have to get a room," Sherri said.

"We have plenty of space here. You're welcome to stay," Bryce said.

"Okay, we'll stay," Kelvin replied, smiling. "Thank you."

Sherri and I went to check on the kids. When we returned, the men were laughing again. Kelvin then said, "Bryce, check this out. A man got lost in the woods. A lion saw the man, got down on his knees, and started to pray. The man saw the lion praying and asked, 'Why are you praying?' The lion looked up at the man and replied, 'I always bless my food before I eat.'" We laughed until we cried.

"Kelvin, you need to go to bed!" Sherri said, laughing hard.

"Wait a minute. Bryce, I have something else to tell you," he said.

"Kelvin! Let them go to bed!"

"No, no. Tell me," Bryce said, still laughing.

"Okay. A girl lived with her grandmother. She asked if she could go out on a date. The grandmother told her she could, but not to disgrace her family. There was a knock at the door. It was the girl's date. Before leaving, the grandmother reminded the girl, 'Don't disgrace our family.' The girl left, and the grandmother waited up for her to return, but she got sleepy and went to bed. The next morning, the girl came downstairs. Grandma asked, 'How was your date? Did you disgrace our family?' The girl said happily, 'No, grandma, I didn't disgrace our family; I disgraced his family.'" We laughed until we cried!

Soon after, we all said goodnight and went to bed. Once Bryce and I settled in for the night, he said, "That Kelvin is something else!"

"Yes, he is. He was like that when he and Sherri were dating," I replied.

He laughed and asked, "Do you want to disgrace my family?" We laughed so hard, we nearly cried ourselves to sleep.

I was up, changing Eric, when Bryce stirred out of his sleep. He climbed out of bed, kissed me on the cheek, and said, "Happy Birthday, Babe! Stay in here until someone comes to get you, okay?" He went into the bathroom, came back out, and reminded me to stay put. He left the bedroom and closed the door behind him. I could tell they were cooking because I could smell the aroma coming from the kitchen.

About 30 minutes later, BJ came to the door and said, "You can come out now, Mama."

As soon as I stepped into the kitchen, everyone yelled, "Happy Birthday!" I looked around and saw they had prepared a big breakfast. There was food spread across the island. "Thank you all for my birthday breakfast," I said, smiling from ear to ear. Ms. Eva came out of the family room. "Ms. Eva! I didn't know you were here, too!"

"She helped us cook!" Kyra said happily.

Just then, Bryce received a text on his phone and excused himself, and my Mama called, FaceTiming me to wish me a happy birthday. "Thank you, Mama. Guess who's here?"

"Who?" I turned my phone around so that she could see Sherri's family and Ms. Eva. "Hi, everybody!" she said, waving wildly. "Listen, I gotta make this quick. Is Bryce back yet?"

"Yes, Mama. He's standing behind me," I replied.

"Bryce, give her the gift, please."

He handed me a box. "Mama, when did you send this?" I asked.

"I didn't send it. It's been there all along. Open it!"

Inside, there was a photo of her, Brandon, and me. "Mama, I love it! This was taken at church when I was fourteen years old," I recalled fondly.

"Yes, it was. Do you see how much Kyra looks like you?" she asked.

"Yes, I do. Thank you, Mama."

"You're welcome. I'll let you all go now so you can enjoy your breakfast. Bye, Eva and Sherri's family. It's nice to see you!" she said before hanging up.

I grabbed a plate, preparing to stack it up with a bit of everything, but Bryce took it away from me. "Amber, relax. It's your birthday. I'll make your plate," he said with a smile.

We all sat around the island, eating and talking. After breakfast, it was time for Sherri and her family to go to the airport. We said our goodbyes, and they left. As Ms. Eva prepared to leave, she gathered all three of our children to take with her. "Ms. Eva, you're taking Eric, too?" I asked, surprised.

"Yes, I am. It's your birthday. Relax. Kyra and I can handle him," she said, winking at Bryce and closing the door behind them.

I knew Bryce was up to something when he said, "Babe, go and rest. I'll clean up the kitchen. I need you to be rested and ready to go somewhere with me around 1:00."

"Where are we going?" I asked.

"It wouldn't be a surprise if I told you," he replied, kissing me on the cheek.

A little after 1:00, we left the house, heading to my surprise. We pulled up to the Marriott Hotel, checked in, and walked down the hall to a suite. When Bryce opened the door, I heard, "Surprise!" I nearly peed myself. After a quick visit to the bathroom, I came out and saw my Mama. "Mama! What are you doing here? I FaceTimed you this morning and thought you were in Virginia!"

"Nope! I was right here, getting things ready for you."

Sherri's family was there as well. "Sherri, I thought you were already on your way back to Baltimore!" I exclaimed.

"No, we came here to wait for you," she said, laughing.

Terry's family, the pastor and his wife, along with some people from our church, were there as well. A few minutes later, Ms. Eva walked in with my children. I was so surprised that I had to sit down. The room was decorated so beautifully. There was finger food and a huge birthday cake. Kelvin also entertained us with his jokes. We had a wonderful time.

By 6:00, everyone was gone. Ms. Eva took the children home with her. Mama left with Sherri's family. It turned out that Sherri's flight didn't leave until Monday morning, so Bryce booked them a room at a hotel near the airport. Mama's flight to Virginia was leaving the following morning as well.

After Bryce and I packed up all my gifts, he said, "Birthday girl, follow me."

"Where are we going now?"

"Ask no questions. Just follow me." With our arms full of gift bags, we got on an elevator and rode it to the top floor, walking down the hallway to the far end. When he opened the door, I stepped into a suite filled with flowers everywhere. A small box with a big red bow sat on the bed. "Open your gift." Inside was a beautiful diamond necklace with a heart-shaped diamond charm. I started to cry tears of joy. Bryce put on a Barry White CD and sang along to the song "Can't Get Enough of Your Love." I sat on the bed, laughing at my husband, who did his best to mimic Barry. I had one of the happiest birthdays ever. For Bryce and me, it was like we were on our honeymoon for the second time.

On Monday afternoon, we picked up the children from Ms. Eva's. Not long after arriving home, my Mama called to let me know she had made it home and said she really enjoyed spending time with me on my birthday. Early that evening, Sherri called and said the same, adding, "I'm glad I was there to see the expression on your face when you saw us in that room. I can't believe we scared the pee out of you!" We laughed for a long time about that. "Oh! Please tell Kyra thanks for the clothes she gave to Shyra." I assured her I would. "Amber, I gotta run. Something is burning on the stove. We'll talk again soon. Bye!" she said, hurriedly ending the call.

One Saturday morning, a couple of weeks later, Bryce got up earlier than usual to meet the painter at the bakery. I got up with him to change and feed baby Eric. After he left, the baby and I fell back asleep. About 30 minutes later, I was awakened by Bryce. "Why are you back so soon? What's wrong?" I asked, concerned.

"Amber, you won't believe this. Look," he said, handing me a bank envelope before lying across the bed.

"Where did you get this from?" I asked, looking inside the envelope and pulling out a stack of money. "Bryce, this is a lot of money!"

"I was removing the tile boxes from the paint cans to get them ready for when the painters arrived. Beneath the tile boxes was a stack of newspapers. When I picked them up, that envelope fell out onto the floor. I looked inside the envelope and saw all that money. I heard the painters coming in, so I slipped it into my pocket, showed them where the paint was, and told them if they needed me, I'd be at home."

"What are you going to do with it?" I asked while counting the money.

He replied, "I'm going to keep it, I guess. How much is there?"

"Honey, you won't believe it. It's $6,500.00!"

He sat up in bed. "Oh, my God! The lady must have set that money aside to pay the men renovating the building. Amber, we gotta pray about this right now." We knelt beside the bed and began to pray.

About five minutes into our prayer, Bryce's cell phone rang, and he put it on speaker. It was one of the painters. He said that as he was placing some boxes into the pantry in the kitchen, he found two cans of paint with writing on the lids. One said "kitchen," and the other was labeled "hallway bathroom." He asked, "Do you want me to use that paint?"

"Yes, please," Bryce replied. He hung up the phone, turned to me, and said, "I didn't know anything about a pantry or that paint. Whatever colors are in those cans will be the colors used for the kitchen and hallway," he said, laughing.

I asked, "How long will it take them to finish painting?"

"Well, there are three of them spray-painting the walls, and another young man following behind to do the touch-ups. They might be done around 4:00 this afternoon. Amber, do you realize the Lord blessed us with that building and everything needed to finish the renovations? The paint, floor tiles, carpet, and commodes. Everything was already there! And now, He has blessed us with the money to pay the workers to complete the job. Next week, the other contractor said he'll install the tiles and carpet. Terry said he'll come and help me install the new commodes."

Someone knocked on our bedroom door. "Come in," I called out.

It was BJ. "I'm ready to eat," he said.

"Wake up your sister, and y'all get dressed. We're going out for breakfast. Call your Grandmama and tell her she's invited to come with us. Let her know we'll pick her up at 9:30 if she wants to go," Bryce said.

We went to Cracker Barrel for breakfast and then headed to the City Farmer's Market to buy fresh fruits and vegetables. We waited in line behind about ten other people to pay for our items. When we reached the front, Mrs. Gleason was sitting behind a table with four different cakes and two sweet potato pies, selling them by the slice for $4.00 each. Ms. Eva walked up, leaned toward her, and whispered, "I was up all yesterday baking this for you, and you're out here selling them. I thought they were for your church. I even gave you a discount." She looked up at Ms. Eva and told her to move because she was holding up the line. Ms. Eva leaned closer and said, "Have a nice day, Mrs. Gleason," with fire in her eyes.

On our way to drop off Ms. Eva at home, she said, "Mrs. Gleason was wrong to do me like that! I let her have each cake and pie for only $12.00, and she's out there selling slices. She's making over $30.00 on each! Did you see the small slices she cut?"

Bryce was cracking up. "Mama, when you get your building, you can sell your cakes by the slice, half, or whole."

I slapped his arm to stop him from talking about the building. "Don't feel bad, Ms. Eva. She's actually advertising for you without realizing it. If anybody asks about the cakes and pies, and she tells the truth, she'll have to tell them where to get them from," I said.

She laughed and replied, "Well, I know one thing: She'll be paying full price if she buys from me again!" As she got out of the SUV at her house, she turned around and said, "Thank y'all for taking me to breakfast and to the market to see Mrs. Gleason selling my cakes and pies." We laughed at what she said and how she said it.

We continued toward home, still laughing about the cake and pie incident, when Kyra said, "Daddy, Mrs. Gleason sold some of my cookies, too. I saw the empty tray."

"Lord! I'm glad Mama didn't see it!" Bryce replied as we pulled into the garage. His phone rang as we got out, and he stayed in the SUV, talking to whoever was on the line. The children and I went inside. A few minutes later, he peeked in and said, "The men are finished painting. I'll be back in a little while." When he returned, he said, "Amber, you won't believe how good that place looks!" He was so excited.

On Monday, my secretary and I reviewed Kyra's manuscript to make sure all the new images were placed correctly. Kyra had already done an excellent job of arranging her recipes and pictures on each page. I then took it to Mrs. Young to read through. "Mrs. Hollinger, this is beautiful! There's nothing more to do. The recipes and pictures are amazing. I will read through it by Friday. There's a publishing and printing company down the street," she said.

"London told me about that. I want to invite both of you to my mother-in-law's birthday party. That's when I will give my daughter her finished cookbook. She and her Grandmama are the ones who've worked hard to make each of the items in the book."

"Absolutely! Thank you for the invite. Just let me know the place and time, and I'll be there," she said.

On Friday, I picked up the manuscript from Mrs. Young and dropped it off at the publishing and printing company during my lunch break. I was told they would have the author's copy finished in four days and that someone would call me when it was ready to be picked up. When I got home, Bryce told me he called the man to lay the tiles and carpet in the building, but his son said the guy was out of town at a funeral in Chicago.

That following Wednesday, I had a preliminary hearing scheduled for 10:00 a.m. After the hearing, I checked my phone and saw I had a missed call from the publishing company. I returned the call and was told the author's copy was ready. I had to be back in court at 2:00, so I asked my secretary to pick it up for me. When the hearing was over, I met my secretary in the hallway. She was so excited about the book and said, "I have already seen it. It's beautiful!" as she handed me the bag. I took it out and flipped through it. It was, indeed, beautiful. I couldn't wait to show Bryce.

I went home, excited about the book. I had to wait a while to share it with Bryce because he, Kyra, and his mother were at BJ's track meet that started at 3:00. Around 6:00, they came back. BJ entered and placed a plate on the island. "Hi, Mama," he said quickly before heading into the family room to play with Eric.

Bryce and Kyra came in, laughing. "Babe, BJ needs a lot of practice. We had to wait almost five minutes for that boy to reach the finish line! People started to leave, and he finally finished. He was limping and holding his side." They kept laughing.

I removed the foil from the plate and saw that Ms. Eva had sent me dinner. "Oh, my goodness. This looks good!"

"Babe, it is delicious!" Kyra agreed, then went to her room.

BJ entered the kitchen, carrying Eric. "Next year, I'm going to do better," he said with determination. Bryce chuckled, and Kyra burst out laughing in her room.

When Kyra came back into the kitchen, she said, "I have been researching online and found out there's a culinary baking and pastry school here in Dallas."

"You still have that on your mind?" Bryce asked.

"Daddy, I'm serious about my future. I want to start online classes during my junior year, and when I graduate, I can enroll in college and complete my hands-on training. With the curriculum I have now, I can graduate from high school early. Then I'll talk to Grandmama about us looking for a building. I can also publish my cookie cookbook at that time. I've been saving my money. Do y'all want to see what I have so far?"

"Yes, I'd love to see what you've done," Bryce commented.

Kyra turned toward her room, took one step, then quickly faced us again. "You know what? Never mind. I changed my mind about letting you see it now. I'll wait until it's published so you can see the finished book."

I sat there thinking, *"The book is already finished. It's in my bedroom, and your daddy is going to be surprised when he sees it."*

Kyra handed Bryce a pamphlet for a cruise and said, "Daddy, you need to take us on a cruise."

"Wait, Kyra. I remember you telling me the two of us should go together," I said.

"Yes, I did say that, Mama, but I think it would be good if we all went as a family."

"Good night, Kyra. You just want to go on another cruise. You're not slick," Bryce replied, laughing. She laughed as she went back to her room.

Later that night, after Bryce took a shower and put Eric in his crib, I grabbed Kyra's cookbook from under my pillow and handed it to him. He looked surprised and asked, "When did you do this?"

"I found her incomplete manuscript on her dresser. Do you remember when she was talking about her pens not being how she left them?" He nodded. "Well, that's because I had taken photos of her manuscript. I then took it to my job and had my secretary and an editor look over it before taking it to get printed."

"Babe, she's going to love it! When we surprise my mom, we can surprise her, too!" he said, pulling me close. The next morning, he left early to let the men into the bakery to install the carpet and floor tiles. When he got back, he told me he had bought some furniture for the building but wanted it to be a surprise.

Friday morning, Bryce dropped the children off at his mom's house since they didn't have school. I dropped the baby off at daycare. Before going to work, I stopped by the publishing company, told them I approved the proof copy, and placed an order for 500 books. As I was getting ready to leave, four of the workers there told me they wanted to order two books each.

When I got to work, London said, "I have already sold ten of the cookbooks to my cousins and sisters. I told them the price was $12.00 each. Is that okay?" She was so excited.

"Yes, that price works. You and Mrs. Young will get a free book. Did I forget to mention that you're invited to the birthday surprise celebration?"

She laughed and replied, "I wouldn't miss it for anything! Thank you for inviting me."

On my way home that afternoon, I stopped by Ms. Eva's house to check on Kyra and BJ. BJ was outside, playing with the dog, and Kyra was helping Ms. Eva in the kitchen. Once again, there were cookies, cakes, and pies everywhere. I had no doubt they would appreciate the building when it was ready. When I prepared to leave, BJ said he was ready to come home. Bryce called to let me know he had already picked up Eric from daycare and was at home waiting for me. "Where are you?" he asked.

"I'm leaving your mom's house now. I have BJ with me."

"Okay. I picked up pizza and a movie for us to watch after dinner." By the time we made it home, Bryce was asleep on the couch, and Eric was playing in his walker.

I yelled, "Bryce! You're asleep, and the baby is wandering around all alone! Anything could have happened to him!"

He started laughing. "I wasn't asleep, Babe. Calm down, please. When I heard you drive into the garage, I pretended to be asleep to see your reaction. I was actually hoping Eric would have been crying when you came in." I picked up a couch pillow and threw it at him. He looked at BJ and said, "Boy, you've been playing with that dog again. Go take a shower and change your clothes before dinner." After BJ walked out, Bryce whispered, "Amber, everything is done in the bakery except for installing the two new commodes. I'm thinking about taking BJ with me the next time so that he can dust and sweep."

"I'm not sure if that's a good idea, Hon. What if he accidentally tells Mama or Kyra about the building?"

"I'm sure he won't, especially when it comes to making money." When BJ returned after his shower, Bryce said, "Now you smell like a young man." That comment led to them horsing around. After they both got tired, Bryce asked BJ, "Do you want to go with me tomorrow and make some money?"

"What do I have to do?"

"Just sweep and dust."

"How much are you going to pay me?"

"If you do a good job, $100.00."

"Wow!" BJ exclaimed. "That's a lot of money!"

"You have to be ready to go at 9:00 tomorrow morning."

"Okay, daddy! I'll be ready!" he said excitedly.

After dinner, we went into the family room to watch the movie. Halfway through, BJ fell asleep, so I told him to go to bed.

When the movie was over, I put Eric in his crib for the night, and Bryce and I went to bed. I was almost asleep when Bryce's phone rang. He put it on speaker. It was Allen calling, letting him know he would be in town next Friday afternoon and would get a hotel near the mall. He also stated that the children would be bringing their sleeping bags so they could sleep in the renovated bakery. "I'll need the keys to get into the building," he said.

"Okay," Bryce replied sleepily.

"Is Amber close by?"

"Yes, she's right here, listening to our conversation."

"Amber," Allen began slowly, "how would you feel if Gail came with us?"

Bryce sat upright in bed. "Allen, I do not want that lady coming here and upsetting my daughter!"

"That won't happen."

I jumped into the conversation. "Allen, it's okay for her to come. Kyra has grown up enough to sit and talk to her."

"Okay. Thanks, Amber. We should be there around 5:00. I'll call before we head over. Oh! I almost forgot. We'll handle the dinner and decorations."

"Great! See you next week!" I said, ending the call.

Bryce turned to look at me. "Babe, do you remember what Kyra said about that side of her family?"

"I do, but she was just upset. She didn't really mean what she said. After all, she still talks to Zoe."

"Okay, Babe. We'll see." That was the last thing he said before I heard soft snoring.

I was awakened Saturday morning by Bryce and BJ in the kitchen, as they were getting ready to leave for the bakery. After they left, I got out of bed, sat at the island to eat breakfast, and reflected on my devotion. I thought about Gail's visit. I couldn't hold her responsible for what Carl didn't tell her about Kyra. She didn't know anything about her granddaughter until the family reunion. "Lord, let this all work out when Ms. Gail gets here," I prayed aloud. Kyra called a bit later to tell me how many cakes and cookies she and her Grandmama had baked and that she was ready to distribute the orders to the ladies when they arrived, so her grandmother wouldn't have to get up. "Kyra, that's nice of you to let her sleep in. I know both of you are tired."

"Mama, wait. I need to tell you something."

"Yes? What is it?"

"Zoe's dad caught her with a boy in her room. He punished her, and she ran away." I sat there, listening to her tell me all about what happened to her sister.

My house phone rang. I looked at the caller ID and saw it was my Mama calling. I interrupted Kyra's chatter and said, "I gotta go, sweetie. Your Grandmama Rita is calling." I talked to her until Sherri called to give me the time for the upcoming women's convention. After talking to her for a while, Bryce and BJ walked in.

Bryce kissed me on the cheek and placed a bucket of KFC on the island. "Let me tell you what your son did." BJ walked past me toward his bedroom, looking sad. "That boy broke Terry's designer glasses."

"He did what? How did he manage to get hold of them?"

"Terry put them on the table in the small room. I specifically told BJ not to touch those glasses. Terry and I were working on the commodes, and when we finished, I was looking for the wrench to tighten the screws. I remembered leaving it on the windowsill after I tightened the knob on the front door. On my way to find the wrench, I saw BJ standing in front of the mirror, making silly faces with the glasses on. I yelled at him for disobeying me, and he jumped. He snatched the glasses off his face and broke them. He had the nerve to say it was my fault because I hollered at him and scared him."

"Oh, my goodness! What did you tell Terry?" I asked.

"I told him the truth, and he said, 'That's okay. The store has one pair left like these. If we hurry, they may still be there.' We walked to the mall, and he was able to get a replacement pair. Babe, do you have any idea how much they cost?" I shook my head no. "They were $150.00! I paid for them and gave him $100 for helping me install the commodes."

"What did you do with the broken glasses?" I asked, giggling at the look on his face.

"I gave them to BJ. And before you ask, no, I didn't pay him for his work." I laughed so hard that tears streamed down my cheeks.

I went to check on BJ. When I entered his room, he was lying across his bed, playing his game with the broken glasses on. "Are you ready to eat?" I asked.

He looked at me through his crooked glasses and said, "No." I walked back out, giggling at how ridiculous my son looked.

On Sunday morning, while getting ready for church, Bryce said, "I miss hearing Kyra's voice in the morning."

"Well, she talked a long time to me yesterday about Zoe."

"What's going on with Zoe?" he asked.

"Believe me, you don't want to know."

When we arrived at church, Kyra came over, hugged us, and said she missed us. BJ said, "You were at Grandmama's house."

"I know, but I still miss y'all."

After church, we headed to Ms. Eva's for dinner and then went home. We all showered, put on our pajamas, and gathered in the family room to watch a movie and snack on popcorn before going to bed.

On Monday morning, we all overslept. The children missed the bus, so Bryce had to take them to school, and I dropped Eric off at daycare. I hurried to get to work on time but got caught in a traffic jam. When I finally arrived, I breathed a sigh of relief upon learning my first trial was postponed. "Thank you, Lord!" I said aloud. My next trial started at 11:30, and it was long and exhausting. I didn't get back to my office until after

2:00. I sat there, eating my lunch and waiting to return to the courtroom for the verdict. Bryce called to remind me about the father-daughter dance that evening, saying Kyra wanted him to wear his uniform. "Well, are you going to wear it?" I asked.

"She wants me to. I guess so."

I laughed and said, "She has you wrapped around her little finger. You know you're going to wear it."

He laughed along with me. "She wants everyone to know her daddy is a Senior Officer in the United States Navy."

An assistant knocked on my door to let me know that the court was back in session. "Bryce, I gotta go. I might be getting home late. I pray I make it before the two of you leave." Thankfully, I made it home in time to see Bryce and Kyra and take pictures of them. Kyra wore a long purple dress with rhinestone accents, and Bryce had on his Navy dress blues. They returned around 11:30. Kyra was so excited that she tried to tell me everything that happened in one breath. I had to tell her to slow down and breathe!

"Daddy, thank you for taking me. I really enjoyed myself."

"Thank you for asking me. I enjoyed myself, too," Bryce replied, hugging her tightly before she went to her room to shower and get ready for bed. He and I settled down for the night, and he shared his perspective on the events. "You know, Babe, I really did enjoy myself tonight. We were the best-dressed, the best dancers, and the best-looking father and daughter in the place!" he said, laughing and acting silly.

After work on Tuesday, Bryce was waiting for me in his car with Eric to take me to see the finished bakery. When I walked in, I nearly fainted. It was absolutely gorgeous! There were pub tables with matching chairs, Bible scriptures Ms. Eva liked on one wall, Kyra's favorite scripture on another, and floor-to-ceiling mirrors on the third wall. In the hallway, Bryce hung the framed picture we painted. Inside the apartment, there was a couch in the living room and a pub table with chairs in the dining area. The bedroom was amazing. As I approached the mirror, I noticed a slit. When I slid the mirror aside, it revealed a hallway leading to another bedroom and a full bathroom. At the end of the hall, a pocket door opened to the kitchen. Bryce was in awe and said, "Wow. I didn't know all this was back here." He checked the back door that opens to the carport. "I'm almost sure the sellers didn't realize all this was back here. There's no way they would have lowered the price if they knew. Look, Babe. They painted back here, too."

"I must admit, when I first saw this building, I didn't believe it could look this good. It looks like a new building, right?"

He laughed and replied, "They did a good job with the renovations. Mama is going to love it." We left and made it to the kids' bus stop just as the bus was pulling up.

Kyra got in and said, "I'm glad y'all came. If not, we would have to walk home in the rain."

"How was your day, guys?" Bryce asked.

"I had a good day," Kyra said. "I have homework in math and science to complete tonight."

"What about you, BJ?" I asked.

"It was okay. I got in trouble for talking, but it wasn't my fault. I was asking my friend for my pencil back, and the teacher said she was going to call y'all because I was disrupting her class."

"She called," Bryce said.

"But daddy, I just asked my friend for my pencil!" he whined.

"We will talk about it later," Bryce replied as we pulled into the garage. When I walked into the house, I smelled food. "I was here long enough to cook," Bryce said, smiling.

Kyra rubbed her stomach. "I'm ready to eat so I can get my homework done and finish my tie blanket."

"You mean you just want to talk to your boyfriend," BJ said, wagging his head at her.

"At least I didn't get in trouble at school!" she countered.

"Stop arguing, you two! And BJ, we're going to have a talk about today before you go to bed," Bryce reminded him.

On Wednesday, I attended a hearing about two sisters arguing over a dog. The judge dismissed the case, telling them to work it out themselves. He said, "This is childish. Your mom and dad would probably be turning over in their graves if they knew how you're acting over a dog. Heck, cut the dog in half. Get out of my courtroom!" That remark elicited laughter from the audience. No sooner than I got back to my office than I received a call informing me that the cookbook order was ready. I immediately left and went to the publishing company to pick up the books. I paid $1,125.00 for 500 copies, which averaged $2.25 each. I thought, *"That's not a bad price."* The company also included ten complimentary copies. Three men loaded the five boxes into my SUV and reminded me they wanted two copies each. I told them I would bring them back on Monday, autographed by the author.

On my way home, I stopped at the grocery store and then threw the groceries into the backseat with the books. When I arrived home, Bryce was sitting on the steps with Eric in his walker. I pulled into the garage, and Bryce came over to open the door for me. He kissed me and asked, "How was your day, Babe?" I told him about the hearing and what the judge said. He laughed hard and replied, "That judge must have thought about what King Solomon told the two mothers to do in the Bible."

"What are you doing home so early?" I asked.

"There was a fire in the building next door to ours, and we got smoked out. They closed the building at noon. I'm off until Monday," he replied as he picked up Eric, and we went into the house.

"No, Hon. Give me Eric. I need you to get the groceries out of the backseat."

He opened the back door and exclaimed, "You got the books!"

"Yes. I wanted to surprise you. There are 510 books in there. Kyra is going to be so surprised! The three men who loaded the boxes said they'd like two copies each, and four of the women who work there asked for two books each, too. On

Monday, after the birthday party, I'm going to take 50 books to work with me, autographed by Kyra."

"You know, she can come to work with me when she doesn't have school. She could sell her books and clean my office. I already told the other officers that my daughter published a cookie cookbook," he said, laughing.

"Did you remember we have parent-teacher conferences tonight?" I asked.

"Yes, Kyra reminded me this morning. That's more money out of my pocket," he joked.

When I entered the kitchen, I saw a bouquet of flowers on the island. "Bryce, they're beautiful! What's the occasion?"

"The occasion is you're my wife, and you are going to disgrace my family tonight," he said, laughing and kissing me. "Amber, you make me so happy. When I'm at work, I can't wait to get home to see your beautiful face."

"Stop it! You're making me blush!"

He kissed me again and asked, "How much did the books cost?"

"$1,125.00. I thought it was going to cost more than that."

"I'm so proud of our daughter. Remember, she has a hope and a future," Bryce said, chuckling. "You can drive my car to work tomorrow, and I'll take the books to the bakery. I'm going to write you a check to cover the cost of the books."

"You don't have to do that."

"Technically, I'm not doing it; the woman we bought the building from is. She paid for the painting, carpeting, tiles, four pub tables and chairs, a sectional couch, the extra bedroom, and a full bathroom we didn't even know was there, and now, Kyra's books with that envelope full of money!" he said, laughing. "Do you realize the only thing I paid for was the dumpster rental? That will be gone tomorrow. And Allen called, asking how much the monthly payment was. I told him, and he said that he and Rachel will make the payments for one year."

My jaw dropped open. "Bryce, he said that?"

"Yes. He said Mama is a mother to us all and that I shouldn't have to do it alone."

"Bryce, that's nobody but the Lord."

"Amen. Yes, it is," he said, hugging me before going into the bedroom.

Just then, Kyra and BJ came in from school. "Mama, I'm going to take a nap before we leave for the parent-teacher conference. I'm tired," Kyra announced.

"I want to tell daddy that I didn't get in trouble today," BJ said with a smile.

After dinner, we went to the school for the meetings. We learned that both children were doing well in their classes. However, BJ's teacher said that after he finishes his work, he talks and disrupts the class. On our ride home, both looked over their report cards and counted how much money their daddy owed them for their As and Bs.

In bed that night, Bryce said, "I'm out $60.00 for Kyra and $25.00 for BJ, but I'm deducting $10.00 from him for talking in class."

On Thursday morning, the kids headed off to school. Bryce and Eric were still asleep when I was getting ready to leave. I kissed Bryce on his forehead, but he surprised me by pulling me back into bed. "Good morning, beautiful."

"Bryce, I thought you were asleep!"

"No. I was just lying here, looking at you."

"Well, Mr. Hollinger, I gotta go to work now."

He kissed me passionately and said, "Call in and tell them your husband is home today and that you need to disgrace his family."

"I'm not calling in to say something like that!" We laughed so hard that we woke up Eric. "Bye, Hon. I'll see you this afternoon."

"I love you. Can't wait for you to get back."

Getting to work, I quickly reviewed my notes for a mediation hearing scheduled for 10:30. The sound of an ambulance siren broke through the silence. I looked out the window and saw the EMTs loading someone into the ambulance and driving away. My secretary called to tell me they were rushing Judge Meyer to the hospital. I immediately prayed for his well-being. After the mediation, my next appointment wasn't until 1:00. I stayed in my office, finished paperwork, and ate my lunch. Bryce called to let me know he dropped off Eric at daycare because he had to meet the men at the bakery to pick up the dumpster.

My 1:00 hearing was moved to a different courtroom due to Judge Meyer's medical emergency. I was familiar with the new judge but didn't know him personally. As I stood and presented my closing arguments, the judge kept glancing at me strangely. Suddenly, he stopped me and said to the man, "You're sentenced to five years. After reviewing your previous cases, I see this is the third time you've been in court this year alone for the same charges. Bailiff, get him out of here!" I thought, *"Wow! That was quick! I didn't even get to finish my closing arguments. And why did the judge keep looking at me like that?"* I went to my office, gathered my belongings, and left for the day. During my ride home, I kept reflecting on how the judge looked at me.

When I got home, Bryce and Eric were asleep. I sat in our bedroom chair, watching the local news on TV with the volume turned down. Bryce woke up and asked, "How long have you been here?"

"About an hour."

"Do you want to lie down with me?"

"No, Bryce. Eric is right there." He chuckled, rolled out of bed, and gently pulled me to lie next to him. We watched the security monitor as the children got off the bus.

Kyra walked in and yelled, "Mama! Daddy! We're home! We had gym today, and I'm tired," as she went to her room.

I walked into the kitchen, and BJ asked, "Where's daddy? I want to tell him I had a good day at school again."

"That's good, BJ. Your daddy is in our bedroom," I said, hugging him.

Bryce exited the room, and BJ told him all about his good day at school. They walked into the family room, continuing their conversation. Bryce called out and asked, "What's for dinner?"

"I'm making lasagna, garlic bread, a salad, and banana pudding for dessert."

"Sounds good to me! Allen just called. They should be here around 6:00. Could you make enough for them, just in case they want something to eat?"

"Of course. I had them in mind when I started cooking." Shortly after, the doorbell rang. "Bryce, they're here!" Bryce answered the door and greeted them. With all the sudden noise, Eric started to cry. "Everybody, have a seat. I'll be right back," I said, leaving to get the baby.

As I hurried to the bedroom, I heard Bryce say, "Amber made lasagna for dinner. If you're hungry, head to the island and make a plate." When I returned with Eric, they were seated around the island, eating. I left the kitchen to get Kyra after handing the baby to Bryce.

I entered her room, only to find she was in a deep sleep, with her hair in disarray. I gently shook her and said, "Kyra, wake up."

She looked up at me and asked, "What time is it?"

"It's 6:20."

"6:20 in the morning?" she asked in a panic.

"No. It's Friday evening."

She laughed and replied, "I must have been exhausted. I'm ready to eat now."

"Kyra, Uncle Allen and Aunt Megan are here." She jumped out of bed and looked in the mirror to fix her hair and clothes. "There's someone else here, too," I said cautiously.

"Who?"

"Your Grandmama, Gail." To my surprise, her facial expression never changed.

"Okay!" she said, fixing her bed and then going out to greet them. When she entered the kitchen, she hugged everyone, including Ms. Gail. "Where are Hannah, Becca, and Aunt Rachel?" she asked.

"Rachel and John are at the hotel. Everyone else went to the mall," Megan answered.

"Are y'all going over to Grandmama's house?" Kyra asked.

"No. We're here to surprise her for her birthday," Allen replied.

"But her birthday's not until Wednesday," Kyra said as she made a plate of food.

"We're going to surprise her tomorrow. That's why we're here," Allen said with a broad smile.

Kyra grabbed her plate and sat next to Ms. Gail. I heard Ms.. Gail say, "You are beautiful, Kyra. Look at all this hair," she said as she gently pushed Kyra's hair away from her face. "It's good to see you, dear." Kyra smiled from ear to ear. "You have a lovely home, Bryce and Amber."

"Thank you. Kyra can give you all a tour when you're finished eating," I said.

After eating, Kyra gave them a tour of the house. "I didn't think Kyra would be quite that accepting of Ms. Gail," Bryce commented.

"I told you she's grown up. We talked, and I let her know it's not Ms. Gail's fault that Carl didn't tell her about Kyra. We prayed about it, and she hasn't said anything else since."

"That's what prayer can do," Allen said. "As many times as he visited Montgomery, I had no idea he was Kyra's father."

"That's because he abandoned her before she was born. He hasn't done anything for her, and she doesn't know him," I replied with obvious disdain for the man.

"Wow. I had no idea," Allen replied. He stood, went into the bathroom, and as he was coming out, he said, "When they get back, I'll be ready to go. I'm tired, although I didn't drive for more than two hours."

"Man, that's old age creeping up on you," Bryce said, laughing. He handed Allen the key to the bakery. "Before you walk in, remember how it looked the first time you saw it. It looks nothing like that now."

Just then, Kyra and the others returned from the house tour. "Your home is lovely. I love the backyard," Ms. Gail said.

"Yes, it is truly lovely," Megan agreed.

Ms. Gail turned to face Kyra. "Thank you for the tour."

"You're welcome," she replied, hugging her grandmother.

Allen called out, "Come on, guys. I'm tired. Thanks to Bryce, I just found out I'm getting old." They all laughed.

We said our goodbyes for the night, and Bryce added, "See y'all tomorrow at 1:00!"

After cleaning the kitchen, I went into Mama's room alone to think. When I got into bed, Bryce and Eric were already asleep. I thanked God for how smoothly things went between Kyra and Ms. Gail, then fell fast asleep.

The next morning, Bryce woke me up, saying, "Breakfast is ready, Babe." After eating, Bryce said, "I better call Mama before she leaves home, and we can't find her for her party. It's going on 11:00 now, and you know she likes to be out and about." He called her and put her on speaker. "Good morning, Mama! How are you feeling today?"

"I'm feeling good, thanks to the good Lord. How's everybody over there?"

"We're all good. Just finished breakfast."

"I had a cup of coffee. I'm going out in a few to get something to eat," she said.

"Mama, stay put. I'm coming to take you out for your birthday. I'll be there to pick you up at 12:45."

"Baby Boy, my birthday isn't until Wednesday! Who's the old one here?" she said, giggling.

"Your birthday falls in the middle of the week, Mama. Amber and I will be at work, and the kids will be in school, so we want to take you out today. Get dressed. Wear that nice outfit Amber and the children got you for Christmas."

"Okay, son. See you at 12:45!"

Immediately after hanging up, he rallied all of us to hurry and get ready. "We can't be late picking up your Grandmama."

As we drove up to Ms. Eva's house, we saw she was waiting at the door. Bryce got out to help her into the SUV. After she spoke to all of us, Kyra said, "Grandmama, I like what you're wearing."

"Your daddy told me to wear this. He's always telling me what to do." We all laughed because we knew she was right. When Bryce turned into the mall parking lot, Ms. Eva looked around confused and asked, "You're taking me to dinner in the mall?"

"Not in the mall, Mama. We're going to that building over there," he replied, pointing to the bakery.

"Oh? They turned that building into a restaurant? There's no sign out there yet," Ms. Eva observed.

Bryce parked near the entrance and said, "Stay here, everyone. Let me go inside to see if our tables are ready."

While we waited, Ms. Eva said, "This is a cute building. I hope the food is good."

I nodded and replied, "I hope so, too. I'm ready to eat."

Bryce returned, opening the doors for us and helping us get out. "They're ready for us."

We walked into the building, ensuring Ms. Eva was the last to enter. "Surprise! Happy birthday!" everyone yelled. Allen, Rachel, and their families came from the back, and Ms. Eva started to cry. "Baby Boy, I'm going to get you!" Everybody huddled around her and hugged her. She was speechless.

"Mama, sit down. You look like you're going to faint," Allen said, guiding her to one of the pub chairs. Ms. Eva sat down and looked around at everyone with tears in her eyes. There were about 30 people in attendance, including family members, the pastor, some of her friends from the church, and people from my job and their families, among others.

Kyra started looking around observantly at how the space was decorated. "Look, Grandmama! That's your favorite scripture on that wall. How did they know?" She then turned to the other wall and said, "That's my favorite scripture on that wall!"

Bryce was smiling as he watched his mother's and Kyra's reactions. "Attention, everyone!" he yelled over the murmur of the guests. "We have an announcement to make. Allen, Rachel, please stand by me." They approached, and Bryce said, "Mama, this building is your birthday gift from us. We thought it was time to get you out of your kitchen and into a larger place." Everybody clapped their hands. Allen handed her the box with the key in it.

Ms. Eva opened the box and stared at the key. "This is my building?" she said with a fresh set of tears streaming down her face.

"Yes, Mama. It's all yours," Bryce replied.

Kyra was crying as well. "Grandmama, you prayed and said the Lord was going to bless you with a building, didn't you?"

"Yes, I sure did. Thank you, Jesus!"

Bryce quieted the crowd, saying, "Amber also has an announcement to make." He stepped to the side so that I could set my bag on the counter.

I pulled the cookbook out of Eric's diaper bag and handed it to Kyra. She stood there, looking at the book. When it finally dawned on her that it was hers, she exclaimed, "This is my cookie cookbook!" Everyone was surprised to learn she had written a book.

"I know," I said, smiling from ear to ear.

She walked over to Ms. Eva. "Grandmama, look! This is my book!" She turned around and ran over to Bryce and me, hugging us tightly. "Thank you! Thank you! Mama, when did you do this?"

"We'll talk about that later," I whispered. "Listen up, everybody! There are over 500 copies of the book here today. You can grab your copies today for only $12.00 each and have them autographed by the author herself, Ms. Kyra Hollinger!" The room erupted in applause. When it died down, I continued. "I also want to take this time to thank my secretary, Ms. London, and my editor, Mrs. Young, for helping me." Kyra showed her appreciation by hugging and thanking them.

"The food is ready!" Rachel yelled.

"I want to see my bakery first," Ms. Eva said, standing and walking toward the back. Some of the crowd accompanied her, while others crowded around Kyra to buy her cookbook and get it signed. When the group returned from the tour of the building, Ms. Eva was in tears again. "I love it! It's beautiful!"

The pastor blessed the food, and then everyone sat around the tables. Rachel asked Kyra to take Ms. Eva her plate first, then everyone else lined up to get theirs. The food was catered from Cracker Barrel, and it was delicious!

Ms. Gail approached our family's table. "Kyra, I'm so proud of you! I'd like to purchase 20 books."

"Thank you, G-mom. I'm sorry that I didn't know you when I wrote my book. I would have added your picture in it, too. You're my first customer," Kyra said smiling.

"I want to give my friends one of your cookbooks and let them know my granddaughter is an author at 14 years old," Ms. Gail said proudly before returning to her table.

Hannah, Jessica, and Denise came over. Hannah said, "Daddy wants 20 books, Kyra. I want you to personalize one for me and write, 'To My Favorite Cousin, Hannah,' so I can show it to my friends and they'll see our pictures from when we were on the cruise."

"Okay," Kyra replied, smiling.

"My mom said she wants 20 books, too. I see our pictures in the book from when we were eating cookies on the cruise," Jessica said, laughing.

Kyra laughed along with her. "Do you remember when I asked that lady for the recipe, and the next day, she gave it to me? That's when I asked her to take a picture of us eating the cookies. She snapped the photo and told us we were four beautiful young girls." They all laughed at the memory as they looked at the pictures in the book.

After everyone finished eating, Rachel brought out the ice cream cake, and we sang "Happy Birthday" to Ms. Eva. When she blew out the candles, BJ asked, "Grandmama, did you make a wish?"

"My wish has already been answered, BJ. God has blessed me with a building," she replied as she cut the first piece of her cake.

By 5:00, all the guests had left. Bryce, Allen, John, and AJ stacked the rented tables and chairs against the wall to be picked up on Monday. The girls cleaned the kitchen, and the boys took out the trash and placed it in the mall's dumpster. When they finished their chores, the young people walked to the mall, while the adults went into the apartment at the back of the bakery to talk and rest.

Suddenly, Kyra appeared in the doorway, startling us. "We thought you went to the mall with the other kids," Ms. Eva said.

"I was autographing my books," she replied. "Mama, Daddy, thank you again for publishing my book."

"You're welcome. You deserve that and more. You're such a big help to us with baby Eric," I said.

She hugged us and said, "I need to go and finish signing the books. Uncle Allen, yours is ready. I'll have Aunt Rachel's and G-mom's books autographed soon."

"What's your CashApp ID?" Allen asked.

"Grandmama has it. She'll give it to you," she replied, walking out. She paused to hug Ms. Eva and said, "I love your bakery, Grandmama."

"It's our bakery, Kyra. Our bakery. Get used to saying that." Kyra smiled one of the biggest smiles I've ever seen, walked out, and closed the door behind her.

Bryce started retelling some of the jokes Kelvin told us. Ms. Eva was laughing so hard, she could hardly sit in her chair. John then told a joke. "A woman went to the doctor to have surgery on her cataracts. When she returned for a checkup, she told the doctor she didn't realize how ugly her husband was until the cataracts were removed." We all laughed until tears were pouring out of our eyes. We joked and talked until the children returned.

A short time later, we left, giving Ms. Eva a moment to lock the bakery's door with her new key. Dropping her off at home, she thanked us again for the building and added, "I have never laughed that much in my life! Thank you all for making my birthday special." Bryce got out of the driver's side and walked her to the front door, hugging her tightly before she disappeared inside. As soon as we got home, everyone showered and went straight to bed.

On Sunday morning, all of Ms. Eva's children and grandchildren joined us at church, along with Ms. Gail. After Kyra and two other girls performed an anointed praise dance, the pastor stood and told the congregation about Ms. Eva's new bakery and encouraged everyone to support her business when it opened. He then held up one of Kyra's books and said, "Kyra Hollinger published this cookbook. Saints, buy a book from her. They're only $12.00, and you can get them autographed. She has grown up in this church, so let's support her. Now, open your Bibles to St. John, Chapter 11. I got a word from the Lord." His sermon title was "Lazarus Isn't Dead, He's Just Sleeping." Leaving the church that day, Kyra had almost 50 names and phone numbers of people interested in buying her cookbook.

Our family met up with Ms. Gail, Allen, Rachel, and their families at the bakery and ate the leftovers from the birthday party. Soon after, they picked up their autographed books and headed back to Montgomery.

On Monday morning, as BJ and Kyra got ready to head out the door for the bus, Kyra grabbed one of her books to show her teachers. Bryce dropped Eric off at the daycare, and I left for work at 11:00 with 50 books: 12 for London, ten for Mrs. Young, and the rest for the employees at the printing shop. Kyra had personalized the ones for London and Mrs. Young, thanking them for their help.

At work, I was told Judge Meyer was still hospitalized and that all my trials would be held in Judge Daskin's courtroom— the same judge who looked at me strangely. That day in court was a repeat. He kept glancing my way throughout the proceedings. When the trial ended, I quickly walked out the door. I heard him call my name, but I pretended not to hear him. I don't know what it was, but he made me feel very uncomfortable. As I left my office that afternoon, preparing to head home, I saw him in the hallway and decided to wait until London was ready to leave. She and I walked out together.

When I got home, the phone was ringing. It was my Mama calling to inform me that Brandon had called, saying he was doing well and wanted her to say hi to me. Kyra said that after showing her book to her teachers, principal, and secretary, they all wanted two copies each. As we ate tacos for dinner, Kyra told us she sold over 200 books that weekend, plus the 16 at school. I told her I sold forty-eight book and would CashApp her the money I had collected.

"Daddy, where's the money I gave you to hold onto yesterday?" she asked.

"In the pants pocket I had on. I'll give it to you when I go into the bedroom," he answered. Later, he called her into the room to give her the money and told her, "The next time you don't have school, I'd like you to come to work with me. You can bring your books to sell and clean my office." She happily agreed to the arrangement, letting him know that Spring Break was coming up in two weeks.

While they were talking, BJ came into our room, crying. "You don't love me anymore. Y'all are always doing stuff for Kyra and don't do anything for me," he whined. Bryce assured him we loved him, and I explained that Kyra wrote her own book; we just published it for her. I hugged him and said, "When Grandmama opens her bakery, you can ask her if you can sell hand-dipped ice cream." That made him happy. He left the room smiling.

Once the kids left the room, I talked to Bryce about the judge and how he watches me all the time. Always optimistic, he said, "Maybe you remind him of someone he knows. What's his name?"

"Judge Daskins. He's a White man, probably in his mid-40s, I'd say."

Let's see what happens tomorrow. If he touches you or says anything inappropriate, I'll talk to him. We can't jump to conclusions based on looks alone," he said, kissing me and playing with my hair.

The next morning, Bryce and the children were already in the kitchen when I got up and got dressed. Breakfast was ready, so we all sat at the island to eat. Kyra was smiling as she said, "Mama, I'm taking 16 books to school today. They have already sent me the money through CashApp."

"That's amazing, Kyra!" I replied. I kissed both of them as they rushed out the door to catch the bus. Bryce and I finished our breakfast, and he kissed me before heading out the door to work. I got Eric ready, dropped him off at daycare, and then went to my job.

I pulled into the parking lot at the same time as Mrs. Young. She got out of her car and asked, "Do you have any books with you?"

"I have two in my office."

"Perfect! I'd like to buy them, please. My husband showed it to his sisters, and they both want one."

"I'll bring them to you at lunchtime," I replied, smiling.

As I headed to my office, I saw Judge Daskins in the hallway, looking my way. I hurried into my office and closed the door. Before I could put my purse down, my phone rang. It was London, telling me that Judge Daskins wanted to meet with me later that morning. "Did he say why?" I asked.

"No, he didn't."

"London, do you know anything about him?"

"The only thing I know is that he's kind of mean and doesn't like it when people enter his courtroom late. Hold on. I have another call coming in." When she got back on the line, she said, "That was the judge, checking to see if you were in your office."

"He knows I'm here. He saw me come in. What did you tell him?"

"I told him you were here but on a call."

"Okay. Thank you, London."

I waited in my office for about ten minutes before walking to Judge Daskins' office. The door was open. I walked in, and he said, "Thanks for coming. Have a seat."

I remained standing and asked, "What is this about, and how long will it take?"

He just sat there, staring at me. His blue eyes traced my face, hair, ears, and neck. I felt violated standing there. He finally asked, "Do you have a meeting this morning?"

"Yes, sir. A new client."

"Well, we'll talk later. I don't want you to be late for your meeting."

"Thank you." I turned and walked back to my office to wait for my client.

At lunch, I gave Mrs. Young the books she asked for and inquired if she knew anything about Judge Daskins. "Not much. He acts weird, looks at people oddly, and is quick to send folks to jail. Why do you ask?"

"I had a meeting with him this morning, and all he did was sit there and stare at me as if he was undressing me with his eyes."

"Really?" She was genuinely shocked. "Be careful when you leave here. In fact, don't walk out alone. Wait for one of us to leave with you."

When I got home that evening, I told Bryce about the incident with the judge in his office. "Did he put his hands on you?" he asked, leaning toward me.

"No. He just looked at me."

"As long as he keeps his distance, I'll keep mine," he replied, hugging me.

Four weeks had passed since the last time I was in Judge Daskins' courtroom, but I saw him watching me periodically when he thought I wasn't looking. One day, I had a trial that ran late. London and Mrs. Young were already gone, so I walked to my vehicle alone. Out of nowhere, Judge Daskins popped out of the shadows and said, "I scared you, didn't I?" He was laughing when he said it.

"Yes, you did. I didn't see you," I replied nervously.

"How's your family?" he asked.

"They're doing great."

"It's good to see you. Have a nice evening," he said as he got into his car and drove off.

My heart was pounding. I had a flashback of when I was kidnapped. I sat in my SUV for a while before leaving because my hands and knees were trembling so badly.

A week later, I had to be at work by 9:00. Once there, I was told my trial was postponed due to a lack of evidence. I thought, *"This is great! I have a short day!"* As I prepared to go home, London called to say that one of the attorneys was ill and left early. They needed a public defender to step in. I walked down to courtroom 'M,' entered, and was handed a folder. I had 15 minutes to review the case before court started.

The case involved a young man accused of stealing a motorbike. When the judge entered the courtroom, he asked if I was there to represent Attorney Halley's client, and I answered yes. The bailiff brought in the young man and handed me a note saying that the boy's father was waiting in the lobby with information about the case. I asked the judge if the father could be brought in from the lobby, and to my surprise, it was Jay Moss. My knees buckled when I saw him, and he had the biggest smile on his face when he saw me. When Jay took the stand, he presented the court with paperwork showing he had purchased the bike for his son. The case was dismissed, and he went back to the lobby to wait for his son's release. While he waited, he spoke with me, stating he didn't know I was a lawyer, and then asked about Mama and Brandon. He also thanked me for getting his son freed from the theft charges.

"I didn't have much to do with that," I replied, smiling. "You had all the legal documents to show the courts, so your son should be thanking you." A few minutes later, his son met him in the lobby, and they left. Jay had his arm happily draped over his son's shoulder.

My workload for the rest of that week was fairly light, so I assisted Ms. Eva in moving some of her belongings into her bakery. On the same day the building passed inspection, she hung her sign outside that read "Eva and Kyra's Bakery and Deli Shop" in bold black letters. At the bottom, in a smaller but still legible font, it said "Soups, Sandwiches, and Hand-Dipped Ice Cream."

The Saturday after she hung her sign, Ms. Eva called us in a panic. "What are y'all doing?" she asked.

"Eating breakfast. What's wrong, Ms. Eva?" I asked. Suddenly, I started to panic, too.

"Are y'all dressed?"

"Yes, ma'am. What's wrong?" I asked again, but louder.

She took a deep breath before replying. "When I drove up to the bakery this morning, there were people waiting to get in. I told them to come back at noon. I need y'all here, right now!" She hung up without giving me a chance to say another word. I told Bryce what she said, and we all got dressed, making it to the bakery around 9:45. When we arrived, people were sitting in their cars, still waiting.

As we walked through the door, Ms. Eva was frantically placing cakes and pies in the showcase. "I haven't even put up the 'Grand Opening' sign, and people are already here!"

Bryce walked over and embraced her, trying to calm her down. "It's okay, Mama. What do you want us to do?" he asked softly.

"Everything," was her blunt response. We laughed at the expression on her face.

We worked quickly to help Ms. Eva get everything in place. "Where are the signs with the prices on them?" Bryce asked.

"I had them laminated, but I didn't bring them in. BJ, can you go get them off the backseat, please?" When he brought them in, we added a picture next to each food item and then posted the signs behind the counter.

"Mama, you have less than an hour before the doors open. Are you ready?" Bryce asked.

"Yes," she said, smiling. "I'm thankful that y'all could come to help me."

"After today, it will be easier for you. Now that the signs are up, the customers can see the prices before placing their orders," Bryce said encouragingly. "Okay, everybody. Listen up. Amber, you're on the register. Kyra, you help your Grandmama. If anyone wants ice cream, I'll dish it up."

BJ looked sad when he asked, "What can I do?"

"For now, just watch me," Bryce instructed. "When it's not busy, you will handle the ice cream. Mama, is the soup ready?"

"Yes, I have chicken, vegetable, and cream of broccoli soups, and everything is fresh and ready for the sandwiches," she replied.

"Grandmama, everything looks good. We have ten minutes before we open!" Kyra said happily.

We stood in a circle and prayed for a smooth opening day. Shortly afterward, Bryce opened the doors and waved in the customers. As the customers poured into the bakery, Ms. Eva would say, "Welcome to Eva and Kyra's Bakery!" There were so many people that Bryce had to limit the number to 20 at a time.

My heart skipped a beat when I saw Jay Moss in line. When he reached the register to pay for his food, he said, "We meet again," then introduced his wife to me. He told her I was the lawyer who got their son out of jail. I smiled and reminded him that he had all the proper papers. He thanked me again, and his wife said, "We'll be back!"

I was happy to see people buying Kyra's cookbook, which was stacked on the counter near the register. A few people recognized me from the courthouse. By 3:00 p.m., we had sold out of everything except for a little bit of soup and bread.

Ms. Eva locked the doors and plopped down onto one of the pub chairs, catching her breath. "I've decided I'm only going to be open Thursday through Saturday from 10:00 to 4:00. That will give me time to buy supplies and bake." She also mentioned she had a call-in order for eight cakes and a dozen each of chocolate chip, oatmeal raisin, and peanut butter cookies for a church luncheon that needed to be ready by Wednesday at 4:00 p.m. "I already made batches of cookie dough and rolled them. All I have to do is take them out of the freezer, cut, and bake."

"Grandmama, don't worry. We can do it with God on our side," Kyra said.

"You're right, Kyra. We did it with one stove, and now we have two plus three ovens. We can do it in half the time!" she replied, hugging Kyra.

"You made a lot of money today, didn't you, Grandmama?" BJ asked.

"Boy, stay out of your grandmother's business!" Bryce said.

Ms. Eva laughed. "BJ, I think we did pretty well." We helped her clean up, and then she said, "I'm hungry and need some real food. Let's all go to Cracker Barrel. Dinner's on me!"

At dinner, Ms. Eva was eating chicken wings and suddenly burst out laughing. "You know, I had four people ask me if I had chicken wings today. I think I'm going to add them to my menu. There's a big deep fryer in the kitchen, just waiting to be used." When Thursday came, she did what she said she was going to do! There were fried chicken wings on the menu— picture included. She hired Ms. Flossie (one of the mothers from the church) to work with her on Thursday and Friday from noon to 3:00. Her job was to make sandwiches, serve soups, and fry chicken wings.

The following Wednesday, while I was driving home, I heard my phone ringing under my seat. It had fallen out of my purse on my way to work, and I couldn't reach it. It was around 1:00 when I picked up Eric from daycare and then went to the bakery to hang out with Ms. Eva until it was time for the children to come home from school. When I arrived, Ms. Eva was getting into her car. I pulled up next to her, and before I could say anything, she yelled, "Why haven't you been answering your phone? Kyra is in the hospital!"

"What happened to her?"

"I'm not sure. I'm on my way there now."

"No, you can ride with me," I said, unlocking the door.

She got in and said, "Baby Boy picked her up from school around 9:00 this morning. She was throwing up, saying her side was hurting and that she was in a lot of pain. Baby Boy said he called you, but you didn't answer. Then he called me. I tried to call you, too, but didn't get an answer either."

"Ms. Eva, my phone is wedged under my seat. It's been there since this morning. I can't reach it." She prayed as I drove. When we made it to the hospital, we were directed to Kyra's recovery room. Walking in, we saw Bryce at her bedside, and BJ was asleep in a chair. "Bryce, what's wrong with her?"

"Babe, she'll be alright. It was her appendix."

The doctor walked in and said, "Y'all have a strong young lady here. After the anesthesiologist gave her the medicine, I asked her to tell me about herself. While the medicine was taking effect, she talked about you guys. Before she went out,

215

she told me she wrote a cookie cookbook, and then she prayed. That was it!" He was laughing so hard. "Okay. Let me get this right. You're in the Navy, you're a lawyer, and this must be Grandmama," he said, pointing to each of us.

"That's correct," Bryce confirmed. "Yes, she is a conversationist, and yes, she did write a book. I'll leave one at the desk for you if you'd like."

"Thank you very much. And she's going to be just fine," the doctor said as he shook Bryce's hand before leaving.

A few minutes later, a young man entered, and Bryce introduced him. "This is Kendrick. He was with Kyra when I arrived at the school. He called his dad to ask if he could come with me, so here he is. His dad works here."

I studied him closely. "Aren't you the young man who was crowned king at homecoming?"

"Yes, ma'am. My dad is coming now. I told him where I was."

Bryce looked at the man heading our way and said, "No way! Titus Alexander, is he your son?"

"Yes, he is," he replied, hugging Bryce.

"Thanks for letting him come to the hospital with me."

"No problem, man." Titus looked around, saw Ms. Eva, and hugged her. Then Bryce introduced him to us.

As the men talked, we heard Kyra say groggily, "Daddy, I didn't forget to pray."

He walked over to her and said, 'Princess, we were all praying for you," as he kissed her on the forehead.

"This is your daughter?" Titus asked, laughing. "I'm the one who gave this young lady her anesthesia."

"We heard about her anesthesia talking moments," Bryce replied, joining Titus' laughter.

"Listen, man. I now know your entire family history, thanks to this young lady!" He laughed and chatted with Bryce for a while longer before he and Kendrick left.

When Bryce was getting ready to leave, I asked him to get my phone from under my seat and to bring me the blue bag. There were about a dozen books in it. "Kyra can autograph one for the doctor," I said. He returned with both, kissed Kyra and me good night, and then left to take his mom and the boys home. Three hours later, he called to check on Kyra before going to bed. "She's resting right now, but the nurses said she's recovering well."

"That's good news. Okay. Love you, Babe. See you in the morning."

Early Thursday morning, Bryce came to visit Kyra. Since she was more awake than when he left the night before, he asked her to autograph a book for the doctor and said he would leave it at the nurse's station for him. He kissed her on the forehead and then went to work. While I was in the bathroom, I heard Kyra talking to someone. When I came out, I saw it was a nurse, telling Kyra she would be released later in the day after the doctor came to see her. I recognized the nurse as Monica Green. We were happy to see each other.

"A man in a Navy uniform said I could come to this room to purchase a cookbook," she said, giggling.

"Yes, that was my husband, Bryce, and this is our daughter, Kyra. She published a cookie cookbook."

"He said the price is $12.00 each. Is that correct?"

"Yes, that's correct."

Monica handed me $60.00 in cash, and Kyra signed five books for her. "Thank you, Nurse Monica. Just so you know, my book is also available on Amazon," Kyra said.

"That's good to know because all my nieces will get one for a Christmas present," she replied, laughing. "Amber, it was good to see you again."

"Same here, Monica. Take care," I said, hugging her. Kyra was released that afternoon.

Monday, the children were out of school for the start of their Spring Break. Wednesday afternoon, Bryce and I got our taxes done. We were happy with the amount of money we were getting back and swung by the house to pick up Ms. Eva and the children. We wanted to celebrate that we didn't have to pay anything back that year. Thursday, Kyra went to work with Bryce, taking her books with her. Eric went to daycare, and BJ went with Ms. Eva to the bakery while I was at work. Around noon, Kyra called to tell me she had sold all 20 books she took with her and that two other officers wanted her to clean and reorganize their offices. "Kyra, you can't do too much. Remember, you just had surgery."

"I know, Mama. There's not much to do. I'll finish both offices this afternoon. Plus, daddy is watching everything I do," she said, laughing.

After work, I picked up Eric and had dinner ready when Bryce and the kids got home. Ms. Eva called a little later, asking Bryce to go to her house, feed the dog, and bring her blow-up mattress, a sheet, pillows, and a blanket. She said she was going to spend the night in the apartment at the bakery. Bryce asked me to go instead, saying he didn't want the dog jumping on him. I asked Kyra to come with me. When we walked into the bakery, Ms. Eva yelled, "Baby Boy, make sure you lock the door behind you!"

"Okay! I will! Ms. Eva, it's Kyra and me!" I called out as we walked back to the apartment.

"Hi, y'all! I've been baking all afternoon. There are cakes in the oven right now."

"Grandmama, can I sleep here with you tonight?" Kyra asked.

"Yes, you can. I just heard the timer go off. Take those cakes out of the oven for me, please."

"Yes, ma'am," Kyra said, walking to the kitchen. "Grandmama, when did you get this big TV?" she yelled.

"This morning. BJ and I went to Walmart, and I bought it. I paid Mr. Al to install it for me. Look in the blue jar next to the mixer and get your money. He bought two of your books."

"Thanks, Grandmama!" When Kyra returned, she asked, "What are you going to put on the cakes I just took out of the oven?"

Ms. Eva told her which icing she would put on each and added, "I baked ten cakes and two poundcakes today. BJ peeled the sweet potatoes for the pies. I'm so happy! I can bake three cakes at a time. I love my bakery and apartment, Amber. Thank y'all so much for getting this building for me."

"Ms. Eva, you deserve all this and more."

She stood, slid the door open, and walked down the hall to the kitchen, saying, "I wonder if Baby Boy can put a pocket door on this wall."

"It looks like a simple fix. I'll ask him when I get home. Okay, BJ, it's time to go. Are you ready?"

"Mama, can I stay here with Grandmama and Kyra?" he asked.

"If your Grandmama says it's okay."

"Yes, he can stay. That way, we'll have a man in the house," she said, smiling.

When I got home, Bryce was reading his Bible, and Eric was asleep. "What took you so long?" he asked.

"I sat and talked with your mom for a while and helped her set up the bed. She asked if you would install a pocket door so she won't have to go through her bedroom to get to her living room."

"Okay. I'll have a look at what she wants done the next time I go over there. Titus called to check on Kyra. We talked for a long time. I told him I think his son is sweet on our daughter."

I laughed and asked, "What did he say?"

"He agreed!" We both had a good laugh at that one.

I went to take a shower. When I got out, Bryce was sitting on the bed. "I just got a call to be in Kansas City on Tuesday of next week."

"Okay. We'll be here when you get back."

He pulled me onto the bed and kissed me. "That's all you're going to say?"

"Well, Bryce, you have to go. There's nothing I could say to make you stay."

He snuggled close to me. "Oh, my God! You smell good. What scent is that?"

"Shower soap." He laughed and kissed me some more.

On Monday afternoon, Bryce left for Kansas City. I told Kyra to get Eric from daycare, and I would get him on Wednesday and Thursday. Friday, I didn't have to go to work. On Friday, the cleaning crew came in to do their monthly cleaning. I waited for the children to get home from school, and then we went to Burger King to get food for everyone, including Ms. Eva. We then went to the bakery. When Ms. Eva saw the bags, she said, "I was just getting ready to run out to grab a bite to eat."

"You don't have to. Here's your dinner," I replied, handing her a bag.

"Thank you. You always seem to know what I want," she said, laughing.

We sat together and ate our dinner. For dessert, we enjoyed scoops of Ms. Eva's ice cream. When it was time for me to go home, I asked, "Who's coming home with me?" Nobody said a word. "Okay! I'll see you guys tomorrow!" I hugged each of them and told Ms. Eva I loved her and that she was the best mother-in-law any woman could have.

"I love you, too, Amber. Ever since the first day I saw you."

I picked up Eric from the walker Ms. Eva kept at her apartment and went home. I quickly put Eric to bed for the night, took a shower, and then sat in bed, reading my Bible until I fell asleep. Around 2:00 a.m., I felt someone kissing my cheek. I jumped and screamed. "Oh, my God! Bryce! I wasn't expecting you until later."

"I wanted to surprise you. I took the last flight out, and here I am! Are the children at Mama's house? I see they're not in their rooms."

"They're at the apartment with her. She's thinking about moving there permanently and turning the carport into a two-car garage."

"Oh, she is?" Bryce asked with his jaw dropped. "Babe, I sold ten of Kyra's books and have eight people's names and numbers. They want Kyra to call them."

"I didn't know you took books with you."

"Actually, they were left in my car. When I got to the airport, I decided to take them with me to see if any of the officers wanted to buy one for their daughters. Babe, are you going to sleep on me?"

"Almost."

"You can't go back to sleep! I just got home," he said, hugging and laughing at me.

On the Saturday of BJ's birthday, we had planned for everyone to go to the zoo with him, but we were very busy at the bakery. Kyra and I couldn't leave, so he and Bryce went without us. When they came back, the bakery was closed, and we had a surprise waiting for BJ. Ms. Eva had asked the parents of three of the boys BJ played with at her house to drop them off at the bakery. He was so surprised to see them there. I gave him an art set, Kyra gave him a high-flying Spiderman action toy, and Ms. Eva baked him a cake with candles. His friends also brought him gifts. After the party, Bryce and BJ took the boys home. I was thankful to God that BJ said he enjoyed his birthday.

While school was out for the summer, I didn't take on any cases at work during August. Every Thursday through Saturday, I helped Ms. Eva at the bakery. During the summer, she sold items from her house and moved into her apartment. She also converted the carport into a two-car garage, just as she wanted.

Months later, Kyra asked to celebrate her 15th birthday early. We planned the celebration for the Saturday before. That Friday night, she stayed with Ms. Eva, helping with decorations and baking cookies. On Saturday, when all ten of her guests arrived, they walked to the mall and went to the movies. Afterward, they returned to the bakery for food, games, cake, and ice cream. Ms. Eva spent the day designing a beautiful ice cream cake, topped with the number 15. Kyra's guests left by 9:00 p.m., and she said she really enjoyed the party.

On Monday afternoon, when Bryce got home from work, he received an emergency call saying they needed him in Omaha, Nebraska, by noon on Wednesday. Sadly, one of the officers was killed in a car accident, and his memorial service was scheduled for the following Tuesday. "When are you leaving?" I asked.

"Tomorrow at 10:20 a.m." He hugged me and said, "I don't want to go. I'm getting too old for this."

"That's what you signed up for, Hon."

"I know, Babe, but all these years, I have never been away on a weekend.

When he mentioned 'weekend,' I said, "Bryce, I'm supposed to be in Baltimore on Sunday."

He stopped packing, looked at me, and replied, "Babe, you know I can't change my orders. Take Kyra with you. I'll call Mama and ask her to keep the boys."

On Tuesday morning, Bryce left early to stop by his office and pick up papers he needed to take to Omaha. On Wednesday night, he called and said, "I've made reservations for you and Kyra. You'll fly out of Dallas at 9:23 Saturday morning and arrive in Baltimore at 12:05. There will be a car waiting to take you to the Hilton Baltimore Suites near the airport. I have already talked to Mama about keeping the boys."

"Bryce, you didn't have to do that. I could have made our reservations and talked to your Mama."

"Babe, you forget that I get military discounts and special privileges. All you two have to do is show your driver's licenses. The rest is taken care of," he said, laughing as we said our goodbyes.

Saturday, we dropped the boys off early at Ms. Eva's to catch our flight on time. When we arrived in Baltimore, I picked up the rental car and drove to the hotel. After checking in, I called Bryce to let him know we had arrived, followed by a call to Sherri to let her know Kyra and I were in town. Later, Kyra and I went sightseeing and looked for a place to eat. We settled on Applebee's. On our way back to the hotel, we got lost. Kyra laughed at me, saying, "We need to call daddy."

"Your dad is in Nebraska. How can he help us? This GPS got us going the wrong way."

She was laughing so hard. "Mama, it told you to turn right, but you turned left." We both laughed together for a long time. We finally found our way back to the hotel. It was after 7:00 p.m. by then. We showered and went to bed.

Early Sunday morning, we had breakfast at the hotel and then headed out to find the church. When we arrived, they had just finished praying. An usher guided us to our seats near the front. I sat down and looked back, noticing how full the church was. Pastor Kelvin announced, "We are happy to have Missionary Amber Hollinger and her daughter Kyra here from Dallas, Texas. Thank you for coming." After the greetings, they continued with the service.

Before Sherri called me to speak, she talked about our friendship and how the Lord was working in my life, sharing that

I was a lawyer and good at my job. She then asked the choir to sing two selections. While they were singing, I saw Kyra say something to the usher, who pointed toward a door. I was sure she was going to change into her praise dance outfit. When the choir finished singing, Kyra entered the sanctuary wearing the outfit her Grandmama bought while on their cruise. I asked if I could use the mic to play the song. The pastor handed it to me, and I played "The Goodness of God." As Kyra danced, the Spirit of God was so high that there was a woman in the back of the church praising Him. People throughout the congregation were standing, including the pastor, Sherri, and members of the choir. When the song ended, people were rejoicing all over the church.

I stood to speak and first thanked God for safe travels for Kyra and me. I then gave honor to Him, Pastor Kelvin, Sherri, and the congregation. I explained that Bryce was on a job assignment in Nebraska and couldn't join us. Then, I shared the scripture I would use for my topic: Psalm 37:4, 'Delight yourself in the Lord...'

"My daughter did a praise dance to 'The Goodness of God,'" I began. "If you listened closely to the words of that song, it was about how faithful God has been to us. Today, I stand before you and ask this question: Has there ever been a time in your life when God hasn't been good to you? In Psalm 38:8, it says, 'O taste and see that the Lord is good and blessed is the man that trusteth in Him.'" I allowed the Lord to speak through me. When I finished, six people approached the altar for prayer. Three of them gave their life to the Lord that day.

After the service, many saints approached Kyra and me, expressing how much they enjoyed the message and the praise dance. We then joined the congregation in the Fellowship Hall for a meal. While eating, Kyra gave Sherri an autographed cookbook. Sherri was surprised to learn she had published a book and shouted over the murmur, "Saints, this is my Goddaughter. She just handed me a cookie cookbook she has published." She held up the book. "It's full of easy-to-read recipes, with pictures of her and her family." Sherri asked Kyra to let them know how they could get a copy of her book. Kyra told them it was on Amazon and that if they wanted an autographed copy, they could contact her and she would mail it to them for $14.00, including shipping and handling. Before lunch was over, 35 people had given Kyra their names and phone numbers, wanting to order books.

As we were getting ready to leave the church, Sherri stopped me and handed me an envelope. "I forgot to give you this. Don't open it until you get back to your room."

Before heading back to the hotel, Kyra and I stopped at the mall. I enjoyed bonding with my daughter. We had fun walking, talking, and laughing. When we got back to the hotel, we had dinner at their restaurant and then went to our room. While Kyra was watching TV, I opened the envelope Sherri gave me. It was a thank you card with a handwritten note that read: "Thank you for being such a good friend. Here is a small token to say how much we love you." She signed it 'The Church, Sherri, and Kelvin,' and added "Call me!" A check for $400.00 was included. I couldn't believe they gave me that amount of money! I called Sherri right away. "Sherri, they didn't have to give me this money!"

"Yes, we did," she said. "We wanted to thank you for the Spirit-filled word you shared with us. My heart is still rejoicing. We're already looking forward to you and Kyra coming back next year, and you better not say no." We both laughed. "Call me when you get home." We ended the call, and I went to bed.

Early Monday morning, we got up, returned the rental car to the airport, and had enough time to sit and eat breakfast before our flight. We arrived back in Dallas at 11:30, stopped by Ms. Eva's, and picked up the boys. Bryce called shortly after we got home, letting me know he would be leaving Nebraska immediately after the officer's memorial service on Tuesday, with his flight scheduled to land at 10:40 p.m. I told him about our trip, and he laughed when I mentioned we got lost and that Kyra suggested I call him to help us. "Bryce, the hearing for the man who kidnapped me is scheduled for Tuesday morning."

"Can you see if it can be postponed until I get back?" he asked.

"I'll be okay," I assured him. We talked until I started to get sleepy.

On Tuesday morning, I sat in the courtroom, waiting for the kidnapper to be brought in. When he entered, I became nervous, remembering how he rubbed my belly and how scared I was locked in that windowless room. I was thankful when the judge sentenced him to 15 years in prison for his crime without me having to testify. I nearly sprinted out of the courtroom, eager to leave that building.

When I arrived at Ms. Eva's, she and Kyra were busy baking. I picked up the boys and headed home, stopping by Big

John's to get food for us. I decided to get combo meals for Ms. Eva and Kyra. They were surprised to see us again, carrying meals for them. Ms. Eva said, "Thank you so much. I love me some Big John's!"

The boys and I made it home, ate our food, prayed, and got ready for bed. Once in bed, I lay there, thinking about the man who kidnapped me as I drifted off to sleep. Around midnight, Bryce woke me up, saying, "I couldn't wait to get back home to you and my children. Where's Eric?"

"He's in the room with BJ. Kyra is at your mom's." He kissed me and went to check on them.

Coming back into the bedroom, he asked, "How did the trial go?" I quickly shared the details. He got into bed, and I turned my back to him. "What's wrong, Babe?" he asked, gently rubbing my arm.

"Bryce, who is Jai Sinclair?"

"Jai? She was one of my classmates. You know her?" he asked.

"No, I don't know her. Why was her number in your pants pocket?"

He sat up in bed and said, "Oh, we were on the same flight to Kansas City. She's a traveling nurse. She bought one of Kyra's books. Babe, she was impressed with the book and told me to have Kyra call her. She wants to arrange something at one of their church meetings. What did you do with the number? I have to give it to Kyra."

"It's in the trash."

He started laughing and kissed me. "Babe, you have nothing to be insecure about. We went to school together. Her last name was Jones back then. She dated Titus and had a baby. That baby is Kendrick." As he was speaking, I fell back asleep.

On Wednesday morning, the boys were so happy to see their daddy when they woke up. BJ told him everything that happened while he was away, while Eric wrapped himself around Bryce's leg. Around noon, we went to the bakery. It was raining hard when we left, and just as hard when we made it to Ms. Eva's. Bryce called his mom, asking her to let the garage door up. As he drove in, he saw Django and said, "She's got that dog over here."

BJ hopped out and rubbed Django on his head. "His house is in the backyard, daddy." Bryce shook his head as we walked under the breezeway into the apartment. The dog followed us. I laughed at the expression Bryce had on his face.

Bryce hugged his mom and said, "Mama, I like your garage. They did a good job attaching it to the breezeway. And I see you've got your dog over here, too."

"Yes, my company-keeper is here," she replied with a smile, looking down at Django.

He turned to Kyra. "Princess, I sold the eight books that were in the bag you left in my car, and I have eight other people's names and phone numbers waiting for you to call them to place orders. They're in my briefcase at home."

Ms. Eva stood and said, "Baby Boy, see the pocket door they put in for me? Come with me and see the big TV in the kitchen." Bryce followed his Mama, carrying Eric with him.

Kyra was sitting at the dining room table, counting her money. "Kyra, you have a lot of money," BJ observed.

"Yes, it's a lot, but I have to use this money to buy more books," she replied.

Just then, I remembered I hadn't called Sherri to let her know we were home. I pulled my phone out of my purse and dialed her number. When she answered, she whispered, "I'm in a meeting. Tell Kyra to add 12 more books to my list and to text me her CashApp ID. Amber, I'm still thinking about the message you gave on Sunday. My heart is still rejoicing. We'll talk later."

When I relayed Sherri's message to Kyra, she said, "I already have orders for 50 books coming from her church."

"Well, add 12 more!" I replied. Kyra was so excited that she ran out of the room to tell Bryce and her Grandmama about her big order from Sherri's church.

A few minutes later, Bryce walked in and said, "Let's go, you guys." He looked out the window. "It's still raining hard. Mama, I'm glad you have a garage." She laughed and tossed the other remote to the garage doors. As we headed out, Django followed us to the car and watched us leave.

Making it home, Bryce handed Kyra the money and the list of book orders from his Nebraska trip. "Did you give her the list from Kansas City?" I asked.

"No, I didn't. Kyra, check my camouflage jacket in the closet. Is there a brown envelope in the right pocket?"

"Yes, here it is," she replied, holding it up.

"It should be cash for ten books and a list with people's names of those wanting books. You need to call them right away to see if they're still interested in receiving a book. I'm so sorry. I forgot all about them."

"Thank you, daddy," she said as she closed the door behind her. A little while later, she knocked on our door and entered the room with a big smile. "I have to send 72 books to Baltimore, 42 to our church, and 24 from daddy's list," she reported.

"Did you call everyone already?" I asked.

"Yes, and some of them wanted two books. Everybody has already sent me their money through CashApp."

"I'm off work for the next four days. Do you need help?" Bryce asked.

"Once I start packing them up, I'll see." Someone texted her. She looked at her phone and said, "It's my father. He said G-mom told him about my book and that he's proud of me. He wants to order 20 copies and asks that I personalize and autograph one for him. He's asking me to sign it as 'Kyra Benson' so that his friends can see his daughter is a published author. How do I personalize his book? Do I say, 'Thanks for donating your sperm, Carl'?"

"Kyra! That's not nice to say!" Bryce said, surprised.

"Well, what do I say?"

"You can say, 'I wish I knew you sooner,' and then sign it 'Kyra.'"

"But daddy, I don't wish that! And I definitely won't be writing Benson on my name." I sat there in silence, breastfeeding Eric and listening to them talk. "Mama, I'm going to cook breakfast in the morning. I saw this breakfast casserole on Facebook that I want to try out on you guys," she said as she left the room.

"Honestly, I feel like she does. Carl hasn't done anything for her. It takes sheer audacity to ask her to personalize a book and write Benson instead of Hollinger. That's rubbish!" I said, getting up to put Eric in his crib. I then went to take a shower.

Bryce came into the bathroom with me. He was laughing when he said, "We can save water by showering together. Let's disgrace both our families tonight."

"You're silly," I responded, laughing along with him.

On Tuesday morning, Kyra prepared the breakfast casserole as planned. We all gathered around the island and ate. BJ was the first to say, "Kyra, this casserole is good!" Bryce and I agreed.

Seemingly out of nowhere, Kyra said, "Daddy, I'm going to write what you suggested in Carl's book, but I really don't want to. Plus, I can't think of anything else to write."

"Be nice to people, and they will be nice to you," he reminded her. She gave him a funny look that made us all laugh.

After breakfast, Bryce said, "Mama wants me to go to her house and take down the bunk beds to put in the extra room at her apartment."

"Daddy, can I come?" BJ asked.

"Yes."

"Can I come, too? I need to start preparing my cookie dough," Kyra said.

"Yes, but I'm going to the house first to get the beds."

As they were getting ready to leave, I told Kyra to ask her dad to stop by Walmart so she could pick up mailing supplies and packing tape. "You also need to go to the bank and deposit all that cash you have."

"If you want me to do all that, let's go!" Bryce said. He kissed the baby and me before leaving. I spent the whole afternoon washing clothes and doing housework. The rest of the week, Bryce was busy cleaning his mom's house and taking things to her apartment. Kyra was busy baking cookies and addressing packages to mail her books.

The Saturday before Labor Day, Ms. Eva had to call Ms. Flossie to help out at the bakery because it was extremely busy. People would leave the mall and end up at the bakery on their way home. One of the customers was Judge Daskins. He entered with a woman I'd never seen before, looking in the showcase and at the prices on the wall. The woman stepped away to talk to Kyra. As the judge stood in line to pay, I noticed him looking at me with a surprised look on his face. When I finished with the ladies in line in front of him, I called out, "Next!"

The judge approached the register and said, "We were leaving the mall and saw the bakery sign. Is this your bakery?"

"No, it's my mother-in-law's. I help out when I'm needed."

"She has a nice selection of baked goods. Everything looks delicious," he said. Just then, the woman he was with walked up, placed one of Kyra's books on the counter, and was eating a cookie Kyra had given her to taste. He turned to her and said, "This is one of the lawyers who works with me."

"I saw your picture in the book," she said, looking at the cookbook.

"Yes, my daughter is the author," I replied.

"That's what she said! This cookie is really good!" she said, smiling. Judge Daskins paid for their purchase and turned to leave.

"Thank you for shopping with us," I said as they walked away.

"See you in court next week!" he replied with a wave.

Ms. Eva had a busy day, taking call-in orders. By the end of the day, she had orders for 12 cakes, six sweet potato pies, four lemon pies, and five dozen cookies—all scheduled for pickup Monday morning. Kyra said, "Grandmama, I have enough cookie dough already made to fill the orders."

"Well, I'll need your help with my cakes!" she replied, laughing.

"I got your back, Grandmama!"

After Ms. Flossie left, we locked the doors, and I went to the office to count the money. A few minutes later, I heard Kyra talking to a woman who said she was looking for the owner. Ms. Eva came out of the kitchen and said, "I'm the owner. I'm sorry, but we're already closed."

The woman looked disappointed. "Please, ma'am. I need to place an order. I have 25 people driving in from Jackson, Mississippi, on Sunday afternoon for our family reunion on Labor Day. I'll pay you half now if you can fill the order. I'd like to have it ready for pick-up on Sunday at 2:00." Ms. Eva called for me to come and take her order. "Thanks for doing this for me on such short notice. I need eight cakes, eight dozen cookies, and 25 sandwiches cut into quarters, please." I tallied the order, she paid half down, and said, "I'll see y'all on Sunday afternoon," as she walked out the door. Ms. Eva and Kyra got busy right away, filling her order.

On Sunday afternoon, the woman came to pick up her order. She didn't realize that chips and pickles were included with the sandwiches and said, "I was going to stop at Kroger to buy chips and pickles, but I see they're already in the bag. Thank you! You saved me a trip." She paid the remaining balance and added a $30.00 tip.

Sunday evening, Ms. Eva and Kyra worked all night to prepare the orders for pickup on Monday. When all the orders were picked up, Ms. Eva said, "Now, I can rest. Amber, believe it or not, I love my job." We all laughed as she sank onto the sofa in her living room.

On Wednesday, the children returned to school. Bryce stayed home with Eric, who had a bad cold, and I went to work. I sat at my desk and thought, *"Kyra is going to the 11th grade, and BJ to the 7th grade. Lord, time is passing by so fast."* After my trial that day, I went straight home. When I arrived, Bryce had dinner ready, but he and Eric were asleep. I stood there, looking at them, and thanked God for my husband and children. I thought, *"Bryce is going to be surprised when he sees what I have planned for his birthday!"*

On Friday, I called Bryce at work and told him that when he gets off, he should head to his mother's apartment, not home. At 4:30, he pulled into his mom's garage. When he opened the door, we all shouted, "Surprise!" I could tell by the look on his face that he was, indeed, surprised. Ms. Eva prepared his favorite dinner, and Kyra made a birthday cake for him and Eric. I then told him I was taking him somewhere special, so we had to run home to change our clothes. I took him to a Staple Singers concert. Afterward, we checked into the Beeman Hotel, where we had dinner. That night in bed, Bryce kept singing songs to me that we heard at the concert, including "I'll Take You There." I enjoyed seeing him happy and knowing he liked his birthday surprise. "Thank you, Babe, for my birthday gift," he said with a big smile.

During the third week of October, Bryce was called to work in Denver, Colorado, for a week. He flew out Sunday afternoon to be sure he would be at work Monday morning. On Thursday, while I was at work, Sherri called to tell me her cousin, Juanita Scott, had died. She asked if she and Shyra could stay with us and said they would arrive on Friday for the memorial service on Saturday in Terrell, Texas. I told her, "Yes, you're both welcome to stay with me. Be sure to bring an empty suitcase. Kyra has clothes she's outgrown for Shyra."

"Okay. We'll see you around 4:00 p.m. on Friday," she replied, ending the call.

I sat there, thinking about Juanita. I remembered her well from our school days and how she laughed at me when Kyra was a baby. That was the night I took Kyra to the movies with me and was asked to leave because she wouldn't stop crying. I also recalled the crush Juanita had on Brandon and cried when she saw him with his girlfriend. She came into my bedroom, crying and saying, "I love him, Amber." A week later, she had a crush on a boy named Dexter. I had to laugh at how much fun we had growing up together.

My thoughts were interrupted when my phone rang. London was calling to tell me that the court was back in session. When I left work that day, I picked up Eric, went home, and waited for the children's bus to arrive so we could go to Ms. Eva's for dinner. When we walked into the bakery, Ms. Eva said, "Dinner is ready!"

Kyra headed to the living room. "I have homework to do. Then I need to get on the computer for my culinary class. I'll eat later."

"Kyra, do you think you're doing too much?" I asked while eating my food.

"I have a schedule, and it's working for me. I always mail my books on Tuesdays when Grandmama and I pick up supplies. I take the books that go to our church on Sunday. The books I have for Carl are already paid for and autographed. I'll send them on Tuesday, along with the books on daddy's list."

BJ had finished eating his food and was outside playing with the dog.

A short time later, Kyra came up to me and said, "Mama, I placed an order for 350 books that should be ready tomorrow. Can you pick them up for me? They've already been paid for." I was so proud of how organized she was.

"Yes, I'll get them during my lunch break. You guys, Aunt Sherri will be here tomorrow for a memorial service on Saturday," I said, picking up Eric and getting ready to leave. "Who's coming home with me?"

"I'll stay here with Grandmama. When I'm done with my homework, I have a few dozen cookies to bake for tomorrow and Saturday," Kyra said.

I walked to the side door and asked BJ if he was coming with me. He replied, "Can I stay here with Kyra?"

Ms. Eva laughed. "They can both stay."

Once at home, I played with Eric for a while and then made sure my mom's room was ready for Sherri. Later, I bathed Eric and got him ready for bed. I rested for about an hour, read my Bible, and then got in the shower. When I got out, my phone was ringing. It was Bryce. "Where have you been?" he asked.

"I was at your mom's place for a while when I got off work. Kyra and BJ wanted to stay, so it's just Eric and me here. If he had anything to say about it, he probably would have stayed at your mom's, too."

Bryce was cracking up. "Babe, I'll be home on Sunday. We have to work on Saturday."

"You've never had to work on Saturdays before. What's going on?" I asked.

"They work one Saturday a month here. It just so happens that Saturday falls while I'm here. I'll call you when I'm leaving. I miss you. I can't wait to get home." I told him about Juanita's passing and that her memorial service is on Saturday. "I'm sorry to hear that. Give Sherri my condolences and let her know I'll be praying for the family. I love you, Babe. Don't forget to say your prayers," he said, laughing as he hung up the phone.

On Friday, I woke up early. I got dressed, did my devotion, and made breakfast. A short time later, it was time to get Eric ready and drop him off at daycare. It started to rain by the time we left. As I pulled up to the daycare, Emma was standing there, waiting for Eric with her umbrella. I felt blessed to be able to leave my baby with someone who loved and cared about him. My first hearing at work that day was at 10:00. Afterward, I went to the publishing house to pick up Kyra's order. While eating my Arby's lunch at my desk, I prepared myself for my trial that afternoon. Sherri called unexpectedly, letting me know she had taken an early flight and was already at my house. I told her to go to the bakery and wait there. I called Ms. Eva to let her know that a friend of mine was coming and asked if it would be okay for her to stay there until I got off work.

"Is she the friend whose cousin passed away?" she asked.

"Yes, ma'am."

While we were talking, she asked, "Does she have a little girl with her?"

"Yes. My friend's name is Sherri, and her daughter is Shyra."

"I see them pulling up now."

"Thank you, Ms. Eva. I'll see you soon." After work, I picked up two pizzas for dinner on my way home. I called Sherri to let her know she could come over and that I'd be waiting for her and Shyra to arrive. While we ate dinner, we talked and reminisced about our classmates, BJ played his video game, and Kyra packed Shyra's luggage with her too-small clothes.

On Saturday morning, the memorial service was scheduled for 11:00. We dropped the children off at Ms. Eva's apartment early, leaving Shyra with Kyra. When we arrived at the church, we found out they had moved the service to the gym at the high school. Walking in, it was crowded. Juanita was well-known in the community and had worked for the school system for over 15 years. The principal and teachers spoke highly of her as pictures of her interacting with students and staff flashed on the wall. At the end of the service, they asked our graduating class to come forward and sing our school song. That's when I saw classmates who had driven or flown in from different states to be there.

After the service, most attendees gathered in the community room for refreshments. I caught up with people I hadn't seen since high school, including Shanna from Chicago and Lynn from Niagara Falls, New York. Shanna, Lynn, Sherri, Juanita, and I were close friends in high school. Juanita was the funny one who kept us laughing. When you saw one of us, you saw all five of us.

As we were standing there, talking to a group of other classmates, Shanna turned to Lynn and said, "Is that Jeff Brown coming this way? That boy was sweet on you back in the day."

"Yes, that's him, but he's married now, and so am I," Lynn replied, laughing. When Jeff walked up, he spoke to all of us, said how good we all looked, and asked Lynn if she had a moment to speak with him. They stepped away to talk.

A short while later, Carl came over with a young man. "Look at this," he said. "The Four Musketeers are together again, minus one." He turned toward Sherri. "I'm sorry for your loss."

"Thank you," she replied.

He then asked if he could talk to me. Sherri and Shanna walked away, talking with some of our other former classmates. "Talk to me about what?" I asked.

He looked at the boy standing next to him. "I want you to meet my son."

"That's not Carlos," I said, confused.

He laughed. "No, this is my oldest son, CJ. I had him when I was seventeen."

"You had a baby when you were seventeen?" I asked, flabbergasted. I looked at the young man. "Is he your father for real?"

"Yes, ma'am. My name is the same as his," he said, smiling. Just then, he heard a woman's voice calling him. He looked around, saw who it was, and said, "I'll catch you later, dad." To me, he said, "It was nice to meet you."

"Nice to meet you, too," I responded.

Carl watched him walk away and turned back to me. "His mother's name is Natasha. She moved here to Terrell. I didn't know she was pregnant."

"Carl, is this what you wanted to talk to me about? I'm not interested in you or your past."

"Well, CJ is coming to Bay City to live with me. I plan to take him to meet my mother. I told her about him, but she's never met him. I'd like Kyra to come up and meet him. We can all drive to Mama's together. I'll send her a ticket."

I couldn't believe the words he just said. "Wait. Did I hear you say you told your Mama about him, yet you didn't care enough to tell her about Kyra? To answer your question, you'll have to call and ask her daddy if she can come."

"She's my daughter. Why do I have to ask him?" he replied, raising his voice.

"She's the daughter you abandoned before she was born, and now you want her to come and meet your son?" I asked, my tone matching his.

"You let her come before."

"I told you at the reunion why I let her come, didn't I?" I then reminded him of what he did to me. He laughed, explaining why he did what he did. "I should have had you locked up," I said angrily. He stood there, speechless. I smiled and said, "It was nice to see you, Carl Benson. Oh, did you receive the books?" I believe my sudden change in attitude confused him.

"Yes," he said with a half-grin on his face.

Before walking away from him, I said, "You know, you're so concerned about what you want that you didn't even ask how Kyra's doing, yet you want her to come and meet your son. She's doing great, Carl Morgan. Like I said, call and ask her daddy if she can come."

I rejoined Sherri, Shanna, and Lynn. Sherri asked, "What did he want?" I told them what he asked me.

"See, you should have dated Jay like your Mama wanted you to," Shanna said. We all laughed hard and long at what she said. They all knew how much my Mama wanted me to date that boy.

"Speaking of Jay, I saw him in court a few months ago. Before that, I hadn't seen him in over 15 years. Then, I saw him again last month at my mother-in-law's bakery. Before y'all ask, yes, he looks good, and he was with his wife," I stated. They all laughed.

"I have an idea," Sherri began. "I think we should all meet together once a year somewhere." We agreed. "I have everybody's number. I'll call you guys and get something planned." I told them about Kyra's cookbook and promised to have her send each of them a copy so that they could see our family photos in the book. "I have mine already. It's really nice," Sherri stated. The other ladies said they'll be waiting for theirs. Not long after, we said our goodbyes and left the building.

On the way home, Sherri and I got caught in a traffic jam for about an hour, and it started to rain. I called Ms. Eva to let her know we were on our way but stuck in traffic. "Take your time.

We're fine," she said. By the time we made it back, the bakery was closed. The younger ones were watching TV, and Kyra was autographing books. We stayed and talked with Ms. Eva for a while. Before leaving, I asked her to pick up Kyra and BJ for Sunday school. The children hugged her, and we left for my house.

After arriving home and getting the children settled, Sherri and I talked about the day's events and the people we saw while sitting in the family room. "I saw you and Carl having an animated discussion. It looked pretty intense from where I stood." She started moving her hands and rolling her neck like she said I did, and we both burst out laughing. I told her what Carl did to me on prom night. "Carl raped you?" she asked with anger flaring in her eyes.

"Yes. That's how I got pregnant with Kyra. I was a virgin until that night."

"Wait a minute, Amber. Just wait. Are you really saying that Carl Benson forced himself on you?"

I nodded yes. "And today, he had the nerve to say I walked around school like I was better than anyone else. When he and his boys made that bet, he told them I would be his 'number one girl.' That's why he asked me to go to the prom. He had it all planned out. When I got pregnant and told him, he didn't believe me. In fact, he laughed and said that none of the other girls he slept with got pregnant."

"Amber, did you tell anybody else?"

"Nobody but Bryce, and now, you." No sooner than I finished that sentence, Kyra walked in, holding up two dresses.

245

"Mama, which one should I wear to church tomorrow?" she asked.

"I like the one on the left, but if you wear it, you need to wear the matching jacket."

"I know, I know. Daddy doesn't want me wearing sleeveless clothes to church." She started laughing and added, "Neither does Grandmama." She came over, hugged both Sherri and me, and said good night.

Once she was out of earshot, Sherri looked at me and said, "Amber, forget about what Carl did to you all those years ago and thank God for your beautiful daughter. Through pain and fear, God blessed you with a beautiful, healthy child. And please, whatever you do, never tell her that she was a product of a rape." We talked for a long time about other things and then went to bed around midnight.

I was awakened around 8:30 the following morning when Bryce called to let me know he would be boarding his flight soon and should be home around noon. I got up and made breakfast so that the children could eat before going to church, and Sherri and Shyra could eat before they left for the airport. Kyra and BJ went to get ready for church. When Kyra came out of her room, she had a backpack full of cookbooks to take with her. Ms. Eva called, saying she was outside, waiting for them.

After eating breakfast Sherri and Shyra prepared to leave soon after. Then Sherri asked, "Did Kyra leave my books here?"

"Yes, she did," I said, pointing to them.

"Okay. I'll CashApp her the money," she said as she picked them up to leave. We said our goodbyes, and they left. "I'll call you when I get home," she yelled from the car as she pulled away.

I was in the family room playing with Eric when Bryce got home. He hugged and kissed us both, then asked, "Where are the children?"

"Your mom picked them up for church."

He pulled me close and said, "Oh, my God. It feels so good to hold you in my arms. Oh! I have the names of ten more people who want Kyra to call them. Put Eric in his bed and come into our room." Lying in bed, I told Bryce about the memorial service and that Carl was there, asking for Kyra to come to Bay City to meet his son. "What did you tell him?"

"I told him to call and talk to you about it." He didn't say anything else, but I could tell he was already thinking about his response to Carl.

It had been two weeks since I last went to work. When I arrived on Monday morning, I saw Judge Daskins in the hallway looking in my direction as I walked into my office. I waved at him and quickly shut the door behind me. I prayed, then reviewed my notes for the two trials I had that afternoon. Bryce called about an hour later, saying some things that made me laugh. As I enjoyed our conversation, I casually spun around in my chair, laughing at what he said. At one point, I spun around and saw Judge Daskins standing in my doorway, listening to my conversation. I jumped when I saw him. "Bryce, I gotta go. I love you." I sat up straight in my chair and asked the judge, "Why are you here?"

He stood there, staring at me and smiling for a few uncomfortable minutes. "I've missed you and wanted to see what you're wearing today."

"Excuse me? Why are you interested in what I'm wearing?"

"Amber, I watch you every day when you come into work. There's no other woman in this entire building who dresses like you."

"Judge Daskins, I'd prefer that you address me as Mrs. Hollinger, not Amber." I looked past him and saw Bryce walking up behind him. "Bryce! What are you doing here?"

The judge turned around and saw him standing there. "I wanted to surprise you and take you out for lunch. I heard a man's voice on the phone, talking about how you are dressed," he responded.

Judge Dasking looked shocked when Bryce said that. I introduced the two men. The judge extended his hand and said, "Nice to meet you. You're in the Navy?"

"Yes, I am," Bryce replied, shaking the judge's hand.

Judge Daskins turned to face me and said, "Mrs. Hollinger, it was nice talking to you. Have a good day." It seemed he couldn't walk away fast enough.

"Why did he leave so suddenly?" I asked.

"Because I caught him hitting on my wife!"

248

I burst out laughing. "Honey, that man is married. I don't want him. I have you, and you are more than enough man for me!"

He laughed and asked, "Are you ready to go?"

"I can't leave. I have two trials this afternoon. One starts at 1:00." I paused and thought about something Bryce said. "Wait. What did you mean when you said that you heard a man's voice on the phone?"

"Your phone didn't hang up. I heard the entire conversation until I ended the call. I didn't like hearing that man talk about liking the way you dress. As a man, I know that's a man's way of hitting on women."

Just then, my office phone rang. It was London calling, saying, "Judge Ashburn's wife was in an accident. He's canceled all cases in his court until next week."

"London, call down and tell the jailer not to bring up inmates #22 and #34. Let him know their cases are canceled because the judge was called away on an emergency. And London, I'm leaving for the day. If you don't have anything else to do, you can leave, too." To Bryce, I said, "Well, I guess I'm done for the day! Let's go eat!"

That night, Kyra's school hosted their National Honor Society banquet, and Kyra was one of the keynote speakers. We dropped the boys off at Ms. Eva's, where she took pictures of us. She said we looked like a picture out of a magazine. When we arrived at the event, Titus, his wife Claire, and Kendrick were there, waiting to be seated. A couple walked in after us and spoke to all of us. Kendrick hugged the woman and then introduced her to us. "This is my mother, Jai."

"I know your mother," Bryce stated. "We went to school together."

Jai stepped forward and shook my hand. "Bryce, your wife is beautiful. Kyra, you're prettier than the pictures in your book. I bought one from your dad."

"Thank you," Kyra replied, smiling.

"This is my husband, Terrance," Jai said. Bryce shook his hand.

Terrance looked at me and asked, "You're a lawyer, correct?"

"Yes, I am."

"My sister, London, is your secretary."

"Now I remember where I saw you before," I said.

A woman walked up and showed us to our seats. I stood and watched as Kyra and Kendrick walked over to where their classmates were sitting. "What are you looking at?" Bryce asked.

"I'm looking at our beautiful daughter. She's growing up so fast."

While dinner was being served, they showed pictures on the monitor of the children and the various activities they participated in at the school. After dinner, one of the administrators spoke and then invited Kyra to discuss the

Biblical Studies course. When she finished, she asked her class to stand and recite Psalm 136. Afterwards, the principal said a few words and then expressed thanks to everyone for coming. We said our goodbyes and headed home.

I called Ms. Eva to let her know we were on our way to pick up the boys. "Just leave them here," she said. "Both of them are asleep. But tell Kyra she has an order of three dozen cookies to make by Saturday for a wedding reception."

The conversation was playing through the SUV's stereo system. "Okay, Grandmama. I heard you. The cookie dough is already made. I prepared four dozen different kinds of cookies yesterday. They are rolled and ready to bake."

Ms. Eva laughed and said, "I declare, girl: You are on the ball!"

Two weeks later, Bryce surprised us with a weekend family Disney cruise funded by our income tax refund. We drove to Galveston, Texas, and boarded the ship on Friday at noon, heading to Cozumel, Mexico. On Saturday morning, when we went to the dining area for breakfast, we were surprised to see Titus and his family there. We glanced at Kyra's face when she saw Kendrick. I looked at Bryce and whispered, "She's 16, Hon."

He frowned, shook his head, and said, "I'm not ready for this."

There was so much for the children to do on the cruise, and they had a fantastic time. On the drive home on Monday, Kyra and BJ talked the entire way, saying how much they enjoyed themselves. Kyra said, "See, daddy? I told you we needed to go on a family cruise! We all enjoyed ourselves, right?"

"Yes, princess. You're right!" he replied.

On Thursday, we all went to the bakery to visit Ms. Eva. While we were gone, she added peach cobbler, banana pudding, fried pork chops, hot dogs, and tossed salad to her menu. Bryce laughed and said, "Mama, we can't leave you alone for one weekend. You've turned your bakery into a restaurant! Can you even do that?" he asked.

"Yes. I'm licensed to sell light foods," she answered.

"Well, since you are licensed... Kyra, bring me some banana pudding, and put a scoop of vanilla ice cream on the side," Bryce said, laughing.

A week later, while I was at work, Bryce called and asked, "What did you do with that ham bone?"

"It's still in the refrigerator. Why?"

"I was thinking about giving it to Django."

"Wait. Bryce, you're at work, thinking about the dog?"

"I didn't want you to throw it away when you can give it to him instead," he replied. I laughed so hard as I hung up the phone. I knew he was starting to love that dog. It had gotten to the point where, when we went to Ms. Eva's apartment, Django would meet us at the car and escort us to the door. Before going inside, Bryce would pat him on the head.

Six months later, in January, Django died of old age. We were all devastated, but I think Ms. Eva and BJ took his death the hardest. Ms. Eva always said Django was her company-keeper and decided to have him buried in a local dog graveyard.

In July, I got a call from Kyra's G-mom, Gail, wanting to order 20 more books. During the call, she asked if it was okay with us if she gave Kyra a car. "It's okay with me. I'll see what her dad says about it," I answered.

"It's a white 2017 Mustang with a red interior and tinted windows. My husband bought it for himself, but he died one year later. It's just sitting here in my garage. Carl drives it when he visits to keep the engine running. I haven't done much for Kyra, and she's my granddaughter, too. Amber, I'm so proud of her. She's the only one of my grandchildren who's doing something with her life. I heard Zoe's pregnant, and Carlos is always getting into trouble," she said sadly.

"Ms. Gail, Bryce just walked in. Let me put him on the phone so you can tell him about the car."

I handed him the phone and heard him saying, "Yes, ma'am, that will be great... Yes, we can fly in and drive it back... Yes, ma'am... No, I won't tell her. You can tell her when she gets there. I'll just tell her it's a father-daughter trip... Thank you, Ms. Gail. I'll tell her to bring the books with her... Okay, goodbye." He was so happy when he ended the call.

"Oh, my God! Did you see what just happened, Bryce?"

He was smiling from ear to ear. "Yes! Look at God! Well, Kyra and I will fly to Montgomery and drive her car back."

"When are you leaving?"

"Ms. Gail wants us to pick it up by the weekend, before the insurance expires at the end of this month. Do you want to come with us?"

"I can't. Who will be here to help your mom in the bakery? Take BJ. He needs to get away. Maybe it will take his mind off the dog. He's been sad ever since Django died."

That Friday morning, Bryce, Kyra, and BJ flew to Montgomery. Eric and I stayed at Ms. Eva's apartment, and I helped her in the bakery. I received a three-way call from Shanna and Lynn that night, and they told me they had received the cookbooks Kyra sent them. Both had new orders for Kyra. I told them I was busy and that Kyra was out of town, but I'd have her call them when she returned.

On Sunday afternoon, Kyra pulled into the driveway in her car. She was so happy! Bryce followed her all the way home from the airport in his car. Bryce told me he and BJ took her car to get an oil change and have the tires rotated on Saturday, giving Kyra time alone with her G-mom. Before getting on the road early Sunday morning, he talked to her about when and where she could go and told her she was not to let her friends drive her car—ever.

In October, we received an invitation to Ms. Gail's retirement dinner. Bryce didn't want to go and said he'd keep the boys. However, he used his veteran air miles discounts for our flight and booked a room for Kyra and me near the airport. He also mentioned that a rental car would be waiting for us when we arrived. Kyra and I flew out to Montgomery Saturday morning, arriving around 11:30. We picked up the rental car, drove to the hotel, changed our clothes, and then headed to the dining hall where the dinner was held.

We arrived early and saw Carlos, Zoe, her baby, Kai, as well as Carl's oldest son, CJ. We were seated, waiting for the event to start, when Carl's sister came in from Atlanta. She was happy to meet Kyra and said, "I'm your Aunt Shawanna. Mama told me how pretty you were. I couldn't wait to meet you."

Kyra smiled and said, "It's nice to meet you."

Shawanna introduced herself to me and stayed there, talking to us. Carl came over, spoke to us, and asked if he could have Bryce's number. "Why do you want my husband's number?" I asked.

"I want to talk to him about the military." I put Bryce's number in his phone. "Thanks," he said, and walked away.

After everyone took their seats, Ms. Gail walked in wearing a beautiful pure white pantsuit. Before taking her seat, we stood and said a prayer. When the program started, each person who wanted to say a few words about Ms. Gail lined up. Each was given three minutes to speak. Afterwards, we lined up for dinner. At the end of the meal, Ms. Gail said a few words and thanked her family and friends for coming to celebrate with her. Before she finished her speech, she asked Kyra to stand. "This is my granddaughter, Kyra, from Dallas. She has published a cookie cookbook." She held it high in the air for everyone to see. "If you'd like a copy, see me." She then looked directly at me and said, "Amber, thank you for coming and bringing Kyra."

I smiled at her and nodded. I thought, *"Had we not gone to that reunion, Ms. Gail would never have known anything about Kyra."* I glanced at Carl. He was sitting there looking like a knot on a log. Every time I see him, I think about what he did to me, but then I think about Kyra and how much of a blessing she's been in my life.

After dinner, I rode home with Allen and Megan, while Kyra drove the rental car to Ms. Gail's so she could spend time with her family. At 9:00 p.m., Kyra picked me up, and we headed back to the hotel. We flew out mid-morning on Sunday to go home. The guys were still at church when we arrived but got there shortly after.

That evening, I snuggled close to Bryce in bed. He said, "Carl called me yesterday."

"I know. He asked me for your number. He said something about wanting to talk to you concerning some military stuff."

"Babe, that wasn't what the call was about. He told me he got stopped by the police in Kyra's car and hid drugs under the floor mat. Then he said that when he went back to his mom's house to get them, she told him she had given the car to Kyra."

I sat straight up in bed. "Drugs?"

"Yes. He asked me to get them out before y'all got back. I threw them in one of the dumpsters by the mall. Amber, it was about 12 small bags of marijuana in a larger Ziploc bag, and three small bags of pills." I sat there in shock, not knowing what to say. "I thank God Kyra didn't look under that floor mat. I called to let him know I disposed of them and that he needed to get to know Jesus. Because if my daughter had gotten stopped by the police driving around with all that mess in that car, I would have gone looking for him, and he would have met Jesus or Satan early."

I laughed and asked, "What did he say?"

"He said, 'Man, I understand. Thanks for doing that for me.' He had the nerve to hang up on me after that! When I finished talking to him, I had to go and pray. I can't believe we drove that car from Montgomery to Dallas with those drugs hidden inside. Oh, my God. What if the police had stopped us? Amber, that's something Kyra never needs to know about." Bryce called out, "Lord, I thank you!"

For Kyra's graduation, Ms. Gail flew in from Montgomery, and my Mama flew in from Hampton. Both of them stayed with us. Kyra was so happy to have all three of her grandmothers present. On Friday night, all three grandmothers collaborated to make gift bags to pass out at Kyra's drive-by open house. On Saturday, the drive-by open house started at 2:00 p.m. It was very enjoyable, and she received a lot of money and gift cards. On Monday morning, Kyra and I drove Ms. Gail and my Mama to the airport. Ms. Gail told Kyra she was welcome to visit anytime and hugged her goodbye.

****

A year later, Bryce finally retired after serving 20 years in the Navy. Since then, he has spent most of his time working with the outreach mission at our church and helping his Mama at the bakery. One thing he did do was keep the promise he made to Kyra years ago: we took a family trip, along with Titus' family, for a week's vacation to Cedar Point in Ohio—the world's biggest amusement park.

Sherri, Lynn, Shanna, and their families met us there. We had a wonderful time and looked forward to meeting up at the Mall of America the following year... just us ladies.

You wouldn't believe who we ran into at the world's biggest amusement park: Carl.

Explore more titles from Dollie James Jamerson

My Mama's Quilt

My Past Versus My Future

www.ingramcontent.com/pod-product-compliance
Lightning Source LLC
Chambersburg PA
CBHW060416180626
46817CB00007B/2596

* 9 7 8 1 7 3 7 0 8 1 6 7 8 *